For fourteen years now *Perry Rhodan* has been acknowledged to be the world's top-selling science fiction series. Originally published in magazine form in Germany, the series has now appeared in hardback and paperback in the States.

Over five hundred *Perry Rhodan* clubs exist on the Continent and *Perry Rhodan* fan conventions are held annually. The first Perry Rhodan film, *SOS From Outer Space,* has now been released in Europe.

The series has sold over 140 million copies in Europe alone.

Also available in the *Perry Rhodan* series

K. H. Scheer

PERRY RHODAN 13

The Immortal
Unknown

Futura Publications Limited
An Orbit Book

An Orbit Book

First published in Great Britain in 1976
by Futura Publications Limited
Copyright © 1972 by Ace Books
An Ace Book, by arrangement with
Arthur Moewig Verlag
This series was created by Karl-Herbert Scheer
and Walter Ernsting, translated by
Wendayne Ackerman and edited by
Forrest J. Ackerman and Frederick Pohl.

ISBN 0 8600 7888 4
This English edition is dedicated to the
Memory of EDWARD E. SMITH, PhD.
Skylark . . . Lensman . . . 'Doc' . . . Fan
Printed in Great Britain by
Richard Clay (The Chaucer Press) Ltd.,
Bungay, Suffolk
Futura Publications Limited
110 Warner Road, London SE5

CONTENTS

ONE

STARDUST TO ... STAR DUST?

Aboard the giant Arkonide spaceship *Stardust II* a whisper materialized in the control room. It reached the sense organs and was transmitted to the reacting brain. It seemed to emanate from Manuel Garand, the engineer, who was on the telecom. His chubby cherubic face shone in amiable content.

Perry Rhodan smiled involuntarily. Garand's appearance seemed beyond reproach. He was the living personification of cool containment, soothing the frayed nerves of the crew.

But his voice – Something about it seemed ... unnatural ... peculiar. Rhodan listened to the soothing whisper until a severe shock suddenly convulsed his body.

A man writhed and groaned in pain in the high-backed pilot's seat. Two hands tried to clutch throbbing lungs. It was senseless, as senseless as the sounds of torment dictated by the unconscious.

'Wherever I look, I see nothing that isn't perfect,' Garand said solemnly.

A rotating mass of light blotted out his face. Only a gray-white spot remained.

Perry Rhodan, Chief of the New Power and Commander of the *Stardust II*, finally freed himself from the chaotic frenzy which gripped his senses during the great transition through hyper-space.

Suddenly everything sobered. He clearly realized where he was – the functional surroundings were not exactly cozy – and what had happened.

As he came out of his daze and opened his eyes, he observed a twisting image. It took a few moments for him to recognize his own face, reflected in the instrument panel. The huge command center of the immense spaceship was real enough.

Reginald Bell, Capt. Klein and Khrest seemed to be still unconscious.

Rhodan's voice returned hoarsely. 'Hello, Garand, are you there? Garand – what were you saying just now?'

The telecom screen remained blank. Manuel Garand, chief engineer of the *Stardust*, had not spoken.

Perry Rhodan managed to shed the last shred of hallucination and once again his mind was completely lucid. His lean face tautened. He murmured under his breath and slowly eased himself out of the pilot's seat.

On the large frontal panel of the circular observation screen a giant sun was shining. It was a flaming blue star of incredible brightness. Even the automatic ray-filter couldn't screen out a considerable amount of hard ultra-violet. Rhodan's eyes began to ache.

Was this Vega? Could this bloated ball of fire be

the sun whose planetary system they had left a short time ago?

Panic surged up in Perry and his face grew pale. Without moving his head he called out for reassurance. 'Reg!'

But Reginald Bell, his closest companion, did not move. Only his broad face twitched under the impulse of his stimulated nerves.

Perry Rhodan – noted from his years in the U.S. Space Force for his remarkable ability of instantaneous decision in response to emergencies – reacted with the mechanical exactitude of a machine.

His hand hit the bright-red alarm button. Even though he couldn't understand the full extent of what had happened, he grasped the situation with sudden clarity.

Something had gone awry despite his careful planning. The hyper-transition, a faster-than-light jump through the fifth dimension, appeared to have been successful. The state of the unconscious men in the command center was not unexpected and could be considered normal under the circumstances. It was quite possible with hyperjumps across 35,000 light-years that the reactivating of completely dematerialized organisms would cause some complications, Rhodan, too, seemed to have been unconscious, but he had recovered somewhat quicker.

Stardust II had been strained to the limit of its capacity. It would have been unreasonable to expect humans to withstand more than that.

Rhodan could wait calmly for the crew to wake up. What seemed to be out of kilter was this shining blue, strongly pulsating giant star which bore a faint resemblance to Vega.

Rhodan's alarm signal had warned of a catastrophic danger. Although his men were still incapacitated, the positronically programmed robots on board the super-battleship sprang immediately into action.

'Determine our position according to transition co-ordinate ground values. Calculate relativity factor of transition time. Survey star in sight. Transmit data. Carry out mass probings, search for possible planets. Stop. Evaluate immediately.'

The ship's robot brain acknowledged receipt of the rapid acoustic programming. The verbal concepts were converted into mathematical symbols in the innards of the giant ship. Thus the positronic brain was fed the correct basic information for its calculations.

Rhodan glanced in passing at the control dials of the super robot. The machine was humming and functioning normally. It would determine faster than an entire team of scientists whether the transition had been indeed successful and investigate the reasons that the strange occurrence had taken place.

Rhodan sank back into the massive pilot seat. The engines of the spaceship – a sphere with a half-mile diameter – rumbled at zero output. Only the power station in sector II was running at full capacity. It had to furnish the electric current for the numerous auxiliary motors and the enormous amounts of energy required for the defense screens of the supergiant. It indicated that the re-entrance maneuver into the normal continuum of four-dimensional space had succeeded without a flaw.

Stardust II raced, approaching the speed of light, toward the still distant sun.

It was suspended on the front screen of the circular observation system in a splendor of unreal radiance. Apparently, mighty explosions were occurring on the star. Ultra-high protuberances seemed to shoot far out into space.

'If this ball of fire doesn't soon turn into a gigantic atom bomb, I'll swallow the whole *Stardust* like a headache pill,' somebody said with a hoarse and scratchy voice.

Rhodan turned around. Bell had quietly awakened. His wide freckled face resembled a faded blotch of color. His rusty bristles of hair rose even higher than usual from his terribly pale forehead.

Bell coughed and the corners of his mouth twitched.

'Any pain?' Rhodan inquired solicitously. 'If so, where at?'

'None,' Bell replied laconically. 'I feel like a tender little rooster who jumped out of the cook's frying pan at the last moment; with plucked feathers, of course. Do you follow me?'

Rhodan grinned fleetingly. That was just like

Bell.

'Everybody's asleep in the neighborhood, huh?' the squat man growled. 'Give me your energy blaster, Chief. I left mine in the gun locker.'

Rhodan's eyes narrowed. Bell displayed a peculiar smile. It was too frozen to look genuine.

'What for?'

Bell creakily got up from the seat of the second astronaut. He gazed at the screen, studied the image of the flaming sun and answered quietly:

'I'm sorry, but I'll have to shoot Pucky. I hope you realize that mouse-beaver's played one of his practical jokes again. At our last transition, which was meant to take us across a relatively small distance of 2,400 light-years to Vega, that creature manipulated the operation with his enormous telekinetic powers so that we jumped 35,000 light-years and were confronted by an intelligent race we didn't have the slightest desire to meet. We lost time, you know, precious, sorely needed time because of an absurd incident in a world which doesn't concern us humans. I maintain that the mouse-beaver has fooled around again just before we made our leap. He simply can't leave it alone; just as I can't forget about eating. It's in his nature.'

'Oh?'

Bell got red in the face and clenched his powerful fists.

'You're taking chances,' he warned. 'You took a fancy to that creature and you don't want to accept the fact that this beast can cause a disaster with his innate passion for playing. I'm going to shoot the rat!'

'He'll make you look down the barrel of your own gun,' Rhodan scoffed. 'Pucky is an intelligent being and don't you forget it. Nobody will be shot on board my ship.'

'Would you condone a mass murderer? This mouse-beaver can destroy the entire vessel. We've got 500 men on board!'

'I'd court-martial a murderer. Pucky isn't responsible for our predicament.'

Rhodan slashed his hand through the air in the direction of the observation screen. The sun slowly grew. The evaluation of the positronic brain had not yet come through.

Over to the right sat Khrest, the chief Arkonide scientist. His tall lean body stooped forward. His face was slightly distorted. Khrest's white hair, a mark of his race, fluoresced in the light from the multi-colored control lamps.

'These Arkonides don't have much resistance,' Rhodan murmured thoughtfully. 'They've passed the climax of their positive development. Their stellar empire falls apart under the hammer blows of the rebellious population of their colonies.'

'We've acquired the knowledge of the Arkonides and that's all that matters,' Bell scowled. 'Khrest set out to find eternal life in our space sector. He was forced to crash-land on the moon where we found him. Then we established the New Power with the aid of his awe-inspiring knowledge. We were able to prevent an atomic war and almost unite all mankind. We've built a super-city in the middle of the Chinese Gobi Desert and have created an ultra-modern industry in the wilderness, applying Arkonide technology. Alright, Chief, I know all that. You're avoiding the subject. We've accomplished all sorts of possible and impossible things, but you can't render a stupid mouse-beaver harmless. Can you?'

Rhodan winced. Capt. Klein regained consciousness. With a moan he straightened up in his seat. His eyes looked glazed.

'Oh . . .' he uttered, still disturbed. That was all.

The ship returned to life. Somebody yelled, loud and shrill, into the telecom that the *Stardust* was racing into a sun. Moments later the air next to Rhodan's pilot-seat began to stir.

Tako Kakuta, the positive mutant with the astounding capability of tele-transportation, materialized out of nowhere. Smiling sweetly, he nodded to the Second Astronaut, who flinched and gasped for air until he became red in the face.

'I'll murder you!' Bell gnashed his teeth. 'One of these days this guy is going to land in my stomach. Has everybody gone crazy around here?'

Rhodan listened to the reports coming in quick succession from all departments as they were ready to function again.

This time Chief Engineer Garand was indeed on the intercom. Very condescendingly he stated his opinion.

'Everything is under control, sir,' he beamed. His high voice sounded jubilant. 'Has any mischief been committed?'

'You see!' Bell exclaimed. 'He has the same suspicion. Maybe that beast can also make that blue giant sun move out of our way!'

Rhodan cut off the telecom connection with the engine control room. Nothing on board the super-battleship seemed to have changed.

Dr Haggard had quietly and unobtrusively entered the command center. He gave Khrest a high-pressure injection in the arm.

'Very unstable,' Haggard said softly. 'Thora hasn't snapped out of it yet. What happened? I've never experienced such a transition.'

'The limit of the hyper-field converter is at about 35,000 light-years. We've taken a risk by doing it in one jump. I won't try it again.'

Haggard – the physician who with his newly developed anti-serum cured the leukemia from which the Arkonide suffered – silently shrugged his shoulders. The commander ought to know best; he had learned everything by hypno-training that the once active and wise Arkonides had created and developed.

'If I only knew where we are,' rasped Klein, who still had trouble speaking. 'Is this Vega?'

As Rhodan was about to call the astronomical section, the alarm sounded. The positronic computer controlling the range-finder automatically set off the warning signal without human assistance.

All heads were suddenly raised and the conversation stopped abruptly. The relaxed atmosphere changed and every muscle in their bodies tensed up.

The co-ordinated team of 500 men quickly sprang into action. Seconds after the first howling of the sirens, the heavily armored hatches were sealed hermetically. The spacious sphere was subdivided into thousands of units leaving no doubt as to its mechanical efficiency. The gigantic Arkonide vessel of the renowned Imperium class could not be destroyed by any single hit.

Far below the command station, which was located at the geometrical center of the sphere, the atomic fusion-reactors of Arkonide origin began to rumble and all power stations rose to peak output.

In the empty, immeasurably large space between the stars the dimensions of a ship were only significant insofar as they could contain in its innards the necessary installations to produce the energy for its engines, weapons and auxiliary machines.

Rhodan observed the bright points of light flashing on his control screen. The gun-turrets of the *Stardust* automatically swung out. On the range-finder screen of Klein's fire control section the first peaked echo-lines became visible.

The calculating machines whirred. It was a seeming chaos of technology in which man played only a minor role.

'Object located in green sector, 86.4 degrees

horizontal, 22.8 degrees vertical,' the mechanical voice of the calculator rattled. Klein pushed the button of the automatic sensor to pinpoint the detected foreign object.

'Fire Control ready!' he calmly reported. Suddenly he had become very alert.

A strange calm settled over all departments. The automatic control devices had done their part, now it was the duty of the Commander to make the final decisions.

Rhodan looked impassively at the front panel of the observation screen. The foreign object located by the sensor, working at a speed faster than light, should be situated ahead to the right and on a plane a little above.

Seconds later the next message came through. The robot-brain had completed its computations.

'Evaluation as requested at 13:52 hours pursuant to programming by Commander. Ship position in Vega system. Transition accomplished. Pulsating star identical with known Vega. Determined with 100% probability that Vega sun is in process of transformation into Nova. Advise against continuing on course of re-emergence. Growth of star proceeds with abnormal speed incompatible with astronomical laws. Stop.'

Bell's eyes popped. He looked across at Rhodan, whose face betrayed deep concern.

'Nova? Vega is supposed to have become a nova in a few weeks? Ridiculous! It can't be. Such a process takes eons.'

Bell looked around as if pleading for help. He barely registered the awakening of the Arkonide scientist. Khrest understood such phenomenons better. His constitution, which differed from terrestrial humans, had presently overcome his frailty.

'Great Imperium!' he whispered, 'I suspected it.' His reddish eyes sought Rhodan's attention.

'How's that?' the commander asked. The sharp lines around his mouth deepened.

'The last riddle of the Unknown threatens to destroy an entire solar system. Vega is an essential reference point for navigating our positions. If this star goes, we'll never locate the planet we want to find. And Vega has been set to explode!'

'And what about the Ferrons living there?' Bell gasped. 'The poor devils will be boiled to death on their molten planets. Their spaceships are no faster than the velocity of light. They'll never be able to escape from the exploding sun. Did the Unknown go mad?'

'We came a little too late,' Rhodan said in a choked voice. 'Much too late. Our wrong transition has cost us weeks. Meanwhile things have happened here. Khrest, will you please work out the course for the eighth planet. Change of course in three minutes. Thank you.'

The 500 men of the ship's crew looked at each other. The triggers of their weapons remained untouched. The previously spotted objects turned out to be Ferronian spaceships. The egg-shaped outlines were unmistakable as was the fact that it was an enormous fleet consisting of 600 units.

'They're fleeing to the outer planets,' Bell moaned. 'What's going on here?'

Rhodan gave no answer. He seemed to know, or at least surmise, what had occurred on great Vega.

Exactly three minutes later the engines of the super-battleship began to roar. The computed change of course required a curve correction of 18 million miles at a velocity close to the speed of light.

Flaming Vega slowly moved out of the front observation screen. Instead, the infinite darkness of inter-galactic space with its multitude of stars took its place. The eighth planet of Vega, Ferrol, was still 4 billion miles distant.

After the course adjustment Rhodan decided to go into a quick transition. Even at close to the speed of light they would have needed seven hours to reach the eighth planet of the immense stellar system.

Space shook as the battleship disappeared in a brilliant burst of light. It was as if there had never been a *Stardust II*.

TWO

OPERATION: DESPERATION

It was the nature of the Arkonide space-structure sensor to register any changes detected in the rigid structure of four-dimensional space with instantaneous impact.

In hyperspace, where totally different laws reigned – which did not include the concept of time – the impact of a forced entry by a body was transmitted without any delay whatsoever.

For this reason John McClears' loud expletives were drowned out by a devastating roar.

The control center of his ship, an auxiliary craft of the *Good Hope* class with a diameter of sixty yards, seemed to turn into a rattling loose tin can. The fine tuner of his range-finder conked out and the entire space-structure sensor threatened to self-destruct under the resounding vibration from the acoustic signal.

McClears' foot was a millisecond later. He kicked the main switch and the droning ceased.

'A structure disturbance?' wondered Lt Everson, his deputy commander on board the auxiliary ship S-3. 'Some zip, wow!'

'Don't drive me nuts, will you!' Capt. McClears snapped.

'I won't,' Everson muttered. Slowly he rolled his

burly body around to the now useless structure sensor.

'O.K.,' he nonchalantly continued, 'let's get this bucket ready for action. Looks as if it won't be long now. And I thought we had chased those lizards out of the Vega system for good! I guess at least ten big ships must have jumped out of hyperspace.'

'Or one that is colossal,' McClears panted. Exhausted, he fell back into his control seat. S-3 had only a crew of ten on board. Nobody expected to get into serious trouble.

McClears was one of those young spacefighter pilots who were drilled and trained to a fine polish by Rhodan. Once it had been his highest ambition to fly a roaring rocketship of the U.S. Space Force to the moon and he did not expect to go beyond that in his fondest dreams; but toward the end of training, circumstances changed so rapidly as Rhodan established the New Power within a period of a few years, that he had soon become one of the first officers of the old, now defunct *Good Hope* under Rhodan's command.

In due course he had arrived in the Vega system and by now had been given the command of a ship which, a few years ago, would have caused him utter amazement. He probably would have regarded his S-3 as a miracle of titanic proportions. A miracle it was indeed. But he had meanwhile realized that it was far too small to be called titanic.

His lips were pressed against the microphone of the faster-than-light telecom.

'McClears to all Guppies, urgent. Evacuation operations to be immediately discontinued. Rendezvous at Ferrol spaceport. Be prepared to start at alarm signal. I must know what is zooming in on us out there. Let's hope it is the Chief. Otherwise we'll have to get ready for the worst. Stop.'

His message was confirmed by the other seven ships. Everywhere on the eighth Vegan planet the rescue operations were interrupted. The armored hatches closed and the engines began to blast.

The local population retreated in headlong flight from the starting crafts. Desperate outbursts followed as they fled to subterranean cities and tunnels, the only remaining places where survival was still feasible.

A ball of fire spewing searing heat and shining blinding light menaced the sky above the planet Ferrol. Ferrol had always suffered from extreme UV rays but it had never been as unbearable as this.

The commanders of the *Stardust*'s eight auxiliary ships had been fully aware that it would be quite impossible to evacuate five billion Ferrons in time. Moreover, the entire system with its forty-two planets was bound to be destroyed if the heretofore quiescent Vega had really changed into a nova.

The Ferronian scientists were deeply disturbed as they conferred about the so-called impossibility. The facts, alas, proved the exact opposite.

McClears, whose craft was stationed at the huge spaceport of Thorta, watched the quick take-off of the other ships on telecom. All transmitters were turned on. It was of the utmost importance to keep in constant communication.

McClears' damp bright-red hair stuck to his perspiring forehead. His orders came quickly and sharply. His irritation was understandable. Before they had left the *Stardust*'s airlocks four weeks ago, Terra time, Perry Rhodan had promoted him to Chief of the Guppies. McClears was dismayed that he now was stuck with the responsibility after Rhodan suddenly disappeared from the scene with the mothership.

Everson grumbled and fiddled around with the Arkonide structure-sensor. His hypno-training had prepared him to understand the functioning of the set.

With a delicate touch he restored the contact of the burned-up end of the cable. The shock of the spark did not bother a man like Everson.

'It works!' he triumphantly exclaimed.

But a fraction of a second later it blew up again. Everson was hurled against the legs of a fighter robot standing in the corner. This time the set just made a short, loud crack. Then it gave up its hyper-frequency ghost despite its special Arkonide material.

'I'll be a son of a gun,' moaned Everson, 'that was a humdinger of a transition. The first time somebody jumped out of the system and now he shows up again from hyper-space. What next? I better get out of this corner.'

McClears rushed over to the communications center. He came just in time to see the lean face with the gray eyes appear on the videoscreen.

'McClears, are you there?' the voice called from the loudspeaker. '*Stardust* to all Guppies wherever they are. My orders for you are to land at once at Thorta spaceport. Be ready to come aboard the *Stardust* without delay. McClears, did you assist in the evacuation of the population?'

'Yes, sir!' McClears jubilantly bellowed into the mike. 'All ships are on Ferrol. I notified the commanders as soon as we monitored your transition, sir.'

'Good for you!' the curt answer came. 'We were detained, never mind why now. I need everyone on board. Any questions?'

McClears had the uncertain feeling that a mad rush of events was about to break loose. Everson got the same impression.

'Yes, one question, sir,' the captain nervously shouted. 'Vega has started to act up like crazy the last thirty-two days, Terra time. It's developing into a nova, sir.'

'Oh!'

McClears was taken aback. Everson started to grin. If that wasn't just like the old man!

'Of course, sir,' McClears muttered. 'We flew every day to the outer planets where the Ferrons maintain some bases. If we now suddenly shove off with the battleship the Thort will have a fit. The ruler is still here. The mean temperature on Ferrol has gone up 30° F. during these last thirty-two days. We can no longer go outside without protective clothing. If we leave here now, we might as well forget about the trade treaty with the Thort, sir.'

'And if we don't leave, that will be the end of the Thort, Capt. McClears,' Rhodan replied impassively. 'Will you please comply with my instructions. I'm going to pay a visit to the Thort. That will be all.'

The connection was cut off. Rhodan acted as if he had been absent only for a few hours.

McClears slowly turned around. The radio technician on duty looked astonished. Everson's eyes were half closed. The men looked at each other till McClears finally drawled:

'What did he mean by that?'

'I don't have the faintest idea; but I suspect that it has something to do with these damn guessing-games he is playing.'

McClears smiled nervously. Then he gradually became more relaxed. The Chief was back again and everything would be all right.

*   *   *

The spherical monster of Arkonide steel and concentrated power raced into the flaming atmosphere of the eighth Vegan planet. Perry Rhodan came in for a direct landing as the Arkonides were wont to do. This meant that he flew straight toward the celestial body without utilizing the braking effect of an elliptical approach. This was made possible only by the quality of the products created by a far superior technology.

The huge battleship started a powerful tornado in the upper strata of the Ferrol atmosphere. White-hot pre-ionized gasses were compressed and forced out at high velocity from the trajectory to the sides of the ultra-energized reflective screen surrounding the vessel. *Stardust II* remained unhampered; there was no heat caused by air friction.

However, a vast vacuum developed behind the gigantic craft where the dislodged gasses furiously plunged in.

The power generators of the super-battleship howled. Rhodan retarded his speed at twelve miles per second, which was enough to effectively brake the battleship suspended in the antigravity field. Unfortunately, he was unable to prevent the perennially hot masses of air of the planet close to the sun from becoming even more heated. This was due to the flaming exhaust of the impulse-energy engine-jets.

Rhodan had good reasons for his haste. The world below him seemed in danger of disintegration.

Thora, the tall Arkonide woman and last descendant of the ruling dynasty of Arkon, stood behind the pilot seat. Her arrogant bearing could not hide the fact that she was torn by her emotions.

Her strange love-hate relationship with Rhodan had begun at the time her exploration cruiser had crash-landed on Luna where it was subsequently destroyed by H-bombs from Earth. Thora had escaped at the last moment in a sixty-yard-wide auxiliary ship of the Guppy class. Since the craft, named *Good Hope*, could not travel the distance of 30,000 light-years to her home on Arkon, she had become dependent on aid by humans.

Her initial hate of Rhodan had gradually diminished. Only on special occasions did her old feelings surface again. Such was the case now.

She was consumed by a deep rage as she stood behind the man whom she had called an underdeveloped barbarian with the brain of a semi-intelligent ape only a few years ago when they had met for the first time. In the interim many things had changed. Rhodan had established – against resistance from all the nations – the sovereign state of the New Power. A major attack from the depths of the Galaxy had been repulsed.

Vast installations had been created on Earth from Arkonide prototypes. Almost a year ago the space-sensors stationed on Pluto had registered a strong space-structure disturbance in the sector of the star Vega twenty-seven light-years away. Overcome with anxiety that superior alien forces had discovered the Earth and with deep concern for the safety of his home world, Rhodan set out in one of the small auxiliary crafts to have a look. This eventually led to a dangerous conflict with the reptilian race of the Topides who were finally dislodged from the Vegan system by ingenious strategy of his Mutant Corps.

Then Khrest's desire to find the secret of cell-conservation was rekindled. To find eternal life had originally been his reason for coming to this distant corner of the Galaxy. His emergency landing on the Moon constituted a severe setback. On the Vegan planets they had discovered traces of the inhabitants of a world who, supposedly, were in possession of the secret of cell-conservation.

Meanwhile it had come to pass that Rhodan was able to conquer one of the Arkonide super-battleships. It was wrested by the mutants from the lizards who in turn had seized it before from the Arkonides.

Since that time Rhodan had been primarily occupied in finding answers to the puzzling questions of an unknown intelligent personality. Someone seemed to consider it of the utmost importance to test the integrity and wisdom of those who were seeking his secrets.

It was a physically and mentally exhausting undertaking which had strained the nerves of his men almost to the breaking-point.

Now that they believed they were close to the discovery of the planet vanished from the Vegan system, they were facing a flaming sun which hardly any longer resembled the star they had seen for the first time less than a year ago.

Thora felt very bitter when she contemplated

the devastating experiences in connection with the cosmic riddles posed by an infinitely superior intelligence. Without the help of the mutants from Rhodan's special corps they would have met certain death on the giant planet Gol. Its pure energy devouring denizens had not given them much of a chance.

And it had not been much better on the desolate world called Vagabond. The mouse-beavers living there were rather amusing and would have been quite harmless in spite of their uncanny telekinetic capabilities had it not been for their irresistible urge to play with everything in their reach. This was a characteristic of the fairly intelligent beings. They started to play with the ship's machinery and eventually with its weapons.

The mouse-beaver Pucky, who had come aboard as a stowaway, caused dire trouble for Rhodan's ship. It was solely Pucky's fault that they had arrived four weeks late in the Vegan system.

Thora pressed her lips together in indignation. She acknowledged Bell's questioning side-glance only with an inimitably disdainful tossback of her head.

If Thora, the commander of the destroyed exploration cruiser, deigned to recognize anyone at all from Terra, it could only be Perry Rhodan. Here she had met a man as hard as rock.

'I'd fly a little faster,' she remarked provocatively. 'Maybe you can destroy a great part of the surface!'

Rhodan's eyebrows moved up. Calmly he passed his instructions to the engine room. Then he looked into Thora's burning eyes. They had a slightly reddish tint which created a strangely contrasting effect with her more white than blond hair. She presented a fascinating appearance.

'Ferrol will survive it,' he replied. 'You'll have to give up the trip you planned. I'll take off again as soon as the auxiliary ships have returned to their hangars.'

'With an Arkonide battleship of the mighty Imperium class,' she scornfully said; 'with a ship that's really mine.'

'You're quite wrong, my dear. Your sleepy compatriots have lost it to the Topides. I've won it from the lizards and put it back into action. As far as the Arkonide empire is concerned, it had already lost *Stardust II* when the invaders took it over. Haven't we already debated this for hours on end?'

Khrest smiled gently as usual. He had sympathy and understanding for both sides. Then he said a little dejectedly:

'Perry, although I've come to this sector of the Galaxy to explore a mysterious planet, I'm now definitely of the opinion that we ought to give up the idea. We've arrived four weeks too late.'

'I meant to teach that mouse-beaver a lesson,' Bell complainingly interjected, 'but I wasn't allowed to.'

He glanced reproachfully at the Commander.

'That has nothing to do with it.' Khrest shook slowly his high-domed head whose non-human brain had the additional gift of a photographic memory.

'We ought to desist, Perry,' Khrest again implored him. 'I'm convinced that it was the unknown mastermind who converted Vega into a nova. We know from sad experience that all solutions of riddles and tasks are conditional in time. Vega is going to explode and we'll thereby lose our hard-found reference point, which means in mathematical terms that we'll never be able to locate the wandering planet.'

The first mountains appeared on the observation screen. They approached at dreadful speed. *Stardust II* still hurtled furiously across Ferrol.

'Even if I didn't want to go through with it. I've no other choice than to make the best of it now, Khrest. Because of our curiosity and ambitious desire to attain nature's greatest biological mystery, Vega has turned into a burning torch. I regret very much that I'm not in a position to save the doomed Ferrons.'

'Underdeveloped creatures!' Thora commented. She reacted again like a true member of the Arkon dynasty. The human attitude seemed very odd to her.

A strong line formed between Rhodan's eyebrows. He retorted sarcastically:

'Thank you very much for your advice, lady. It happens to be the nature of humans to help when it's possible. We're a little different in this respect. My conscience demands that I do everything to save the threatened Ferrons. The Vegan planets will melt away as soon as the star erupts. We still have some time left even though it involves an artificially caused process which is running a million times faster than a natural occurrence. The only way to help the Ferrons will be to solve our last task.'

'Which is what?' Thora demanded in a hostile tone.

'Locating the vanished planet which – according to the evaluation by the robot-brain – traverses the Galaxy on a fixed course.'

'You're mad! No planet can exist without a sun.'

Now Rhodan countered with empathy in his voice.

'Thora, you're a superb scientist. You must have noticed long ago that we're dealing here with some-one in possession of the most highly accomplished technology in the universe. These beings have discovered the inner-most secrets of nature. Even with the scientific knowledge of the Arkonides I'm unable, utterly unable, to transform such an enormous star into a nova. These unknown beings are far superior to us.'

'You're quite right there. Superior, that is, to the terrestrial barbarians.'

Rhodan suddenly grinned. She was playing that old cracked record again as she always did when she ran out of logical arguments.

'Of course, I must agree,' he sighed. 'Only strange that these barbarians have so quickly mastered your Arkonide technology, isn't it?'

'Touchdown in two minutes,' the automatic navigator announced. The drone of the engines became even louder. The super-battleship thundered at a steep angle toward the spaceport which already could be seen below. Thora finally remained silent.

Due to the anti-distortion field absorbing the deceleration they were not impeded in their movements by the braking maneuver.

'Don't try to slam the door!' Bell shouted after her as she left. 'It's thirty-six inches of solid armorplate.'

Khrest lowered his head. The ill-fated trip to the Earth's solar system had become the worst disappointment of his life. The human race was too young, too adventurous and eager to learn, to be fully appreciated by the descendant of a degenerating race. Nevertheless, Khrest endeavored to practice tolerance. He had for some time realized that mankind was about ready to assume the heritage of the Great Imperium. Men like Rhodan seemed to be predestined. They scorned compromise and had an unlimited thirst for knowledge. They had a great capacity to stand up under painful reverses, and it looked as if a race of such men was made to rule the world. The Arkonides had long lost those talents which their ancestors, too, had possessed many years ago. But this was now ancient history.

Stardust II came down like a giant falling meteor. Only a few feet above the ground was its velocity fully retarded. The impulse waves from the mammoth engines in the ring around the middle of the hull churned up the ground and large molten puddles formed under the heat. The huge pads of the telescoped landing-legs buried themselves noisily in the rock-hard synthetic surface of the spaceport.

Stardust II had returned to the first cosmic trading base of the human race. Twenty-seven light-years separated the vast Vega system from the home world. However, this presented no problem for vessels of the *Stardust*'s class.

The engines came to rest but the whirlwind was still to come.

Searing pressure waves roared with such force across the surface of the spaceport that smaller Ferronian crafts were torn from their take-off ramps. The super-battleship was once again a grandiose mountain of perfect harmony suddenly transplanted on the landing field.

The men in the auxiliary ships of the *Good Hope* class, which had already arrived in the meantime, ducked instinctively. The supergiant had set down precisely within the marked field.

Lt Everson readjusted the observation screen to normal. He did it with a feeling of resignation. Gradually and carefully he turned the step-switch of the optical magnifier to the right. However, he was unable to bring the *Stardust*, which had come down over 500 yards away, into full view on his screen. All he could see was a section of the shiny metallic sphere measuring 2,500 feet in diameter, its mass blocking out the sight of everything else.

'Now we've been downgraded to grasshoppers again,' he said weakly. 'What the heck, but only a few moments ago we really thought we had some colossal spaceships here ourselves. A little depressing, isn't it?'

He glanced at Capt. McClears who was hastily putting on his best uniform.

'Am I glad that the old man has come back!' grunted McClears. 'Man, give me a hand!'

'I'm hungry,' Everson complained. 'During such a state of biological dependence I feel quite incapacitated. The zipper is one eighth of an inch from your fingertips.'

McClears swore horribly. The heavy-set lieutenant nodded solicitously.

'You said it,' he agreed in a sepulchral tone of voice. 'You'll never reach that zipper. We'll have to get a telekinetic mutant.'

'Come and help me!' the captain roared in disgust. 'I'll have to get aboard immediately. The old man will chew me out something awful if I don't show up within five minutes.'

'That would be more than I could bear,' Everson mused loudly. 'Okay, step a little closer. I can't get up right now.'

Grinning from ear to ear Everson relished McClears' voluble imprecations. Perry Rhodan had used very good judgment when he selected his men to serve on board the greatest spaceship of all times. These dare-devils remained unperturbed under any conditions except when they were given nothing to do.

Everson and McClears represented a typical example of the spirit among the spacefighter force. They were constantly ribbing each other murderously but fused together like one brain when the going got tough. That was all that mattered!

*　　　*　　　*

The eight auxiliary ships were hauled aboard with well-trained ease. The super-battleship had swallowed the mighty spacespheres as smoothly as a dinosaur gulping an unwary mud-fish. The Guppies were strictly auxiliary ships.

About fifteen minutes after their arrival the Thort of Ferrol announced his visit. The wise ruler of the far-flung planet system still did not know that Rhodan was an Earthling. Owing to the tremendous technical power at his command he was presumed to be a sovereign agent of the Great Imperium. Only in this manner had Rhodan been able to secure a psychological advantage for his negotiations.

The Ferrons excelled the humans in most respects and could not have been induced to conclude a trade treaty with Earth had they known the true situation there.

The Thort sat down in the imposing command

center of the super-battleship. He was of small but muscular stature and could not hide the ravages the recent events had wreaked on his body. The pale-blue skin of his tiny face had taken on a pitiful gray tone. He had become old and stooped under his burden of worrisome troubles.

His deep-set eyes were hardly discernible. Rhodan was plagued by self-reproach when he caught sight of the Thort. The Ferron feared the extinction of his race.

'What do you propose to do?' he asked dejectedly. 'Will you assist us in our evacuation with your mothership?'

The attending members of the Great Council of Science looked hopefully at the tall lean man in the unadorned uniform. Rhodan knew that his answer was bound to sadden their expectations. He paused and cleared his throat. The officers of *Stardust II* pretended to be indifferent.

John Marshall, one of the most talented mutants in the special corps, unobtrusively probed the mind of the Ferronian ruler. It was easy for the accomplished telepath to divine the thoughts of the alien intelligence. The Thort was strictly preoccupied with the fate of his race. He did not contemplate any devious actions.

'Everything is alright,' Marshall inaudibly informed Rhodan. Rhodan received the telepathic message from brain to brain as a soft whisper.

Still trying to control his emotions, Rhodan began by pointing out:

'Any effort to evacuate the population would be senseless. Even the big vessel is not sufficient to move out the population from the three inhabited planets of your empire. The outer planets, which are up to now little affected by the nova, will also disintegrate when the explosion occurs. Where shall I take your people?'

The old Ferron helplessly stretched out his open hands.

'I put my trust in you. I don't know where.'

'Sir, your sun will explode like a bomb in about three weeks Ferrol time. Please regard my arguments as factual. There is only one solution, which is to normalize the star again. However, this is not in my own power. But I'll find ways and means to spare you from the worst.'

The Thort sat up. He raised his stooped shoulders. 'Ways and means?' he repeated hopefully. 'What possibilities do you have in mind?'

'I know exactly where the source of the trouble can be found. I want to take off without delay. Please refrain from continuing the evacuation which is far beyond the capacity of your space-fleet. Every Ferron you transport to the outer planets will be in a hostile environment bereft of the comforts of your high civilization and technology. You'll condemn your people to death. Remain here and wait!'

'He'll ask you a question,' Marshall warned, just before the Thort posed his inquiry.

'I must beg your indulgence,' Rhodan declined

firmly. 'I regret that I'm not at liberty to divulge where the perpetrator of this conflagration will be found. But I can promise you to find him. You can depend on me.'

When the Thort left, Rhodan saluted him smartly and correctly with all due honors.

As soon as the armored hatch had closed behind the despairing Ferronian ruler, Reginald Bell took a deep breath.

'I feel like crying,' he muttered, heart-broken. 'We'll never find the secret of eternal life. Why did we have to get the Ferrons into such a predicament? It really wasn't necessary.'

'I agree with you for once, barbarian,' Thora said acrimoniously.

Incensed, Bell jumped around. Someone in the background laughed so shrilly that Rhodan's tense face suddenly relaxed. No normal person would have dared to laugh in this tension-ridden situation.

'Barbarian is right,' a high-pitched voice chirped. 'He was out to do me in, that bully. Upon my word of honor, I haven't played with anything this time. I haven't even had so little fun as to let a screw fly through the air.'

Rhodan's lips began to twitch suspiciously. His officers had to apply considerable will power to retain their discipline. They stood like statues. Only Maj. Deringhouse grinned.

'How do you do, your honor,' Rhodan said, keeping his composure. 'Where did you pick up that expression?'

Once again Pucky gave out with the grating shrill sound he called laughter. Then the misshapen mishap of a mouse's imitation waddled out from behind the second stereo-corrector, designed for the precise matching of photographed navigating stars with prefabricated high-accuracy micro-templates.

Pucky, as the intelligent furry animal from the planet Vagabond had been named, seemed to have trouble moving his fat rear-end, with its spoon-shaped beaver-tail, across the floor.

He was about three feet tall and usually walked upright. He was very clever and had the innate gift for telekinetic transportation. As a consequence of his passion for playing, far exceeding human characteristics, he had brought *Stardust II* to the brink of disaster.

But in doing so, he had meant no harm. It was just his irresistible urge to play with these new and wonderful gadgets.

Pucky slowly approached closer with circumspection, swinging around his short forepaws, with their dainty gripping extremities, like a fat-bellied wrestling champion.

He wrinkled his shiny black, mouse-like nose and bared a front tooth in a rosy moist opening.

His tiny paw touched his furry forehead. Rhodan could barely control himself. Now the little mouse-keteer even saluted him.

'Lt Puck of the Mutant Corps reporting ready for action,' the little furball whistled, with an air of looking very important. 'Permit me, sir, not to say Pucky. It seems inappropriate to my honorable new position.'

Rhodan turned around to conceal the laughter which convulsed him. The other men grimaced with distorted faces. Only Bell ran through the whole range of his invectives and gruesome curses which Pucky countered by showing him his front tooth again.

'Assassin!' the bright little creature cussed. 'You wanted to murder me. I've heard you. It wasn't me who played with the sun or with the ship. I gave the Chief my word that I wouldn't play havoc with the levers or swish around without his permission.'

Pucky paused longingly to savor the idea.

'Wouldn't it be fun to swish around! I could direct the ship by remote control of the emergency lever.'

'Swishful thinking!' Bell harrumphed. 'You'll be asking for it if you don't control yourself. By the way, what do you mean, Lt Puck of the Mutant Corps? Since when have you been promoted to officer?'

Pucky turned demonstratively around and smacked the floor with his broad tail. This was a gesture of utter contempt.

'That's for you, Mr Bell,' he chirped devastatingly. 'Phew!'

'Make ship ready to start!' Rhodan's commanding voice broke up the hubbub. 'What's there to

giggle at? Every intelligent being has its peculiar-
ities which we have to respect as tolerant people.
Or aren't you tolerant?'

Rhodan looked coldly around at his officers, who
suddenly froze. This broke him up and he started
to laugh uproariously.

By the Great Imperium of the Arkonides – they
had never seen their Chief act like this before!
Pucky was splendidly amused. He looked almost
tenderly toward the man who understood him so
excellently. It had indeed been a very good idea
to leave the planet Vagabond and slip aboard the
Stardust in that packing case.

Furthermore, when Pucky had been given the
opportunity to learn the principal language of the
humans by hypno-training, it was enough for him
to make a little god out of Perry Rhodan.

The Chief of the New Power ended his laughter
as quickly as he had begun it. Momentarily, the
serious, troubled look returned to his eyes.

'Now, having enjoyed this little diversion, gentle-
men, how about returning to your stations?' Rhodan suggested. 'Khrest, how far did you get with the
evaluation by the positronic computer?'

They all put Pucky out of their minds at once.
The men to whom positronic evaluation was a
meaningful concept, fastened their eyes on the Arkonide scientist.

Khrest gave the impression of erudite confidence.
His white shiny hair reflected a thousandfold the
bright light of the command center.

'I've worked on it for four weeks, Terra time. The exact data concerning the movement of Vega have been fed into the computer. By taking into account the cosmic trajectory, velocity and ancillary data, it will be possible to calculate the probable position of the elusive planet within about two hours. The probable position!' Khrest cautioned.

Garand's rosy face appeared on one of the numerous screens. The engine control room was ready for the launching.

Rhodan looked at the chronometer. It was exactly 17:58 ship time.

'Start at 18:00 o'clock!' Rhodan ordered. 'Pucky, you stay with me. I expect you not to play any tricks now that you're an officer of the Mutant Corps. But you have my permission to play with the First Officer.'

Pucky was in stitches as Reginald Bell's face paled. Rhodan quickly suppressed his grin.

Exactly at 18:00 hours the impulse-drive engines began to blaze. Flaming heat waves scorched the ground. Ominous droning shook the spaceport.

The gigantic body rose vertically from the landing field and raced with such enormous acceleration toward empty space that the atmosphere of Ferrol burned white-hot along its track.

Seconds later *Stardust II* had disappeared. Only stormy winds were left behind as sign of a feat which had been accomplished by a matchless technology.

The Ferrons had neither comparable pressure-shock neutralizers nor energized deflection screens to ward off gas molecules. A Ferronian spaceship could not have started or landed in a similar manner. Besides, their quantum-drive engines were unsuitable for such acceleration despite their unsurpassed quality.

Ferrol had reached the limit of its potentialities. A better performance could not be achieved with their machinery. The inevitable result was a stagnation which had commenced about 1,000 terrestrial years ago. Improvement of details served only to increase reliability. Perry Rhodan was singularly impressed by their fine workmanship. Whatever these people built or manufactured was of sublime quality and deserved the highest praise. The planetary empire of the Thort was a valuable and plentiful resource which Rhodan endeavored to make accessible for use on Earth by concluding a trade treaty.

The last pressure waves faded out. Minutes later they received the message that the Thort had rescinded his evacuation order.

The Ferronian pilots shut down their engines. It ended an operation conceived in desperation and wishful thinking. The human visitors had left the eighth world of Vega behind.

THREE

RHODAN'S DESTINY

The mean solar distance of the planet Ferrol was – according to Ferronian data – 1.1 billion miles.

Since Vega was the indispensable fixation point in the three-dimensional co-ordinate system, Rhodan deemed it necessary – contrary to other opinions – to fly by the star that had turned into an atomic furnace. His reasoning could very well be sound. On the other hand it might be negligible or completely irrelevant. After considering the final evaluation of the positronic computer, he came to the conclusion that no additional tolerances could be permitted which would affect the complicated transition operation. In any case, there were already more than enough unknown factors among the assumptions for the calculations.

Therefore, he opposed risking a transition 1.1 billion miles from Vega. These 1.1 billion miles could easily become 110 billion miles under a tiny hyper-shift which – together with other minimal mistakes in tolerances – could lead to by-passing the planet without light, resulting in total failure.

Khrest thought that the mass-sensor of the battleship would be sensitive enough to detect a body in space at a distance as far as half a light-year away, regardless of whether it was lit by a sun or not.

Rhodan and Khrest thoroughly debated the alternatives. Meanwhile Bell had attained the velocity of light with maximal acceleration. At present the ship raced in free fall toward the blazing sun.

Magnetic storms of tremendous magnitude raged in the high-tension protection screens. Finely spread particles of matter began to concentrate before the screen. The sphere of Arkonide steel was now surrounded by a glowing aureole.

Vega seemed to radiate its mass away. It was destructing itself by spewing immeasurable quantities into space.

All stations aboard the ship were fully manned. Since no battle alert had been ordered, the pilots of the spacefighter squadron and the eight auxiliary ships were doubling as guards for the most important installations. It was an odd and unusual struggle Perry Rhodan dared in his pursuit of utmost accuracy.

The strong gravitational pull of Vega went unnoticed at the velocity with which the *Stardust* was moving. However, the cosmic micro-matter became denser and denser. There were also extensive clouds of gas which, despite their low density, became a danger at their tremendously fast pace.

Rhodan had switched off the various defense screens with the exception of the ionization deflection screen whose greatest energy density was concentrated at the front of the craft as directed by the field-projectors.

Some of the power reserves of the engines were

already used by the chief engineer. Since their
hasty start Garand calculated only in rough figures
beginning at one million to upwards of 250 million
kilowatt-hours per power station.

The leading astronauts and technicians of the
super-battleship maintained silence. Only their
eyes seemed to be alive in their tense faces as they
scrutinized the readings of their instruments.

Next to Rhodan was a console receiving the final
signals from the giant computer of the *Stardust*.
The data determined by the robot-brain were sent
to the command center by optical and audio trans-
mission.

Rhodan's fingertips rested on the still-secured
impulse switch for triggering the transition.

The precisely computed point of departure was
74 million miles from Vega. When *Stardust II*
arrived at that position, the star had to be right on
the beam at 91.3 degrees in the green sector.

As the spaceship passed the trajectory of the first
planet, they caught sight on the videoscreen for a
few moments of its glowing, almost molten body.
This satellite had a mean solar distance of 137
million miles.

In the constellation of their far away home world
it corresponded approximately to the value for the
rather cold Mars. Here, at a comparable distance,
a whole world was a burning hell due to the size
of the central star. Everything in the Vegan sector
was on a titanic scale.

The battleship kept racing on its flight. When

the heavily armored spherical hull began to drone after another light-minute, Rhodan coughed slightly.

'May I have a cup of coffee, Anne? There should be some in the dispenser.'

Anne Sloane, the slim delicate mutant girl with the gift of psychokinesis, did not blink an eyelash.

She concentrated her parapsychological powers on the dispenser. A cup detached itself from the container and floated under the faucet. Without touching the release, the coffee began to flow into the cup whereupon it drifted, as if carried by ghostly hands, toward Rhodan. He took it matter-of-factly. These uncanny tricks of his highly qualified specialists were regarded as common after many such shared experiences.

Anne relaxed the fixed gaze in her eyes and Rhodan thanked her in his most amiable manner.

The droning of the outer hull grew louder and blinding lightning began to flash against the deflection screen.

The taut faces of his men remained motionless. They knew their boss. When he embarked on a nerve-racking adventure they had to keep their composure with a stiff upper lip. No one on board the *Stardust* would have admitted any fear at such times. They talked about everything else except the imminent peril they faced and were apt to crack wacky jokes during the moments before the fatal decision.

The ship began to vibrate. Three more light-minutes till the point of transition. Far below the men's feet the power reactors reached their highest pitch, pouring out the last reserves. Seconds seemed to stretch into eternities.

'Nice weather we're having out there, but it looks a little cloudy,' Bell commented calmly.

Rhodan looked in fascination at the video-screens where a pitilessly raging hell could be seen. The shaking became so wild that the safety harnesses automatically snapped shut around their shoulders.

'Looks like rain,' Rhodan agreed.

Garand's face appeared again on the control screen. His angelic smile was frozen. He reported in an unmodulated tone:

'Engine Control to Commander. We're slowing down a little. Very dense matter retarding our ship. Shall we go?'

'Let her have it!' Rhodan answered, sipping his coffee.

Again the droning of the gigantic ship's engines rose to a crescendo. In order to maintain the necessary speed for the 5-D leap, they were running the engines at 92.8564% of the available thrust.

A shrill wailing sound transformed the space-faring protagonists into humans again. Rhodan turned around. All of a sudden the immutable expression was gone. A gray face with flickering eyes appeared.

'I'm scared!' Pucky squealed. 'I'm terribly frightened.'

Crying for help, he hobbled closer on all fours. Bell laughed loudly.

'Who isn't?' he sympathized. 'One doesn't have to be inhuman to admit it. In two minutes the protective screen is going to collapse, damn it. It will make mincemeat out of us.'

His words were like a signal. Garand started to shout and all the others fell in.

Rhodan sat tensely at the controls. Khrest pressed his clenched fists against his mouth. He stared madly at the pulsating raging monster of a star which still filled the screen although it was already far over to the side. Spectacular gas flames billowed into space from terrific explosions. The *Stardust* skirted the outer limits of the inferno.

Only Rhodan could hear the final communication from the astro-robot. The blue control-lamp flashed faster and faster until its light became constant at its brightest hue.

It was at this moment that Rhodan's brain fleetingly relived the events which led to his search for the greatest mystery of the universe.

It had started innocuously with the discovery of the five-dimensional matter-transmitter. The Ferrons, limited as their knowledge of mathematics had remained, had not mastered the art of constructing such transmitters.

They had discovered the presence of an enigmatic being and were immediately confronted with his first demands. In the end these tasks included parapsychological problems and were solved one by one.

On Pucky's home world the last clue to the existence of a wandering planet was revealed. In the middle of an otherwise empty hall a replica of a galactic section appeared.

Vega was clearly recognizable. Since Rhodan knew definitely that this star was previously circled by forty-three planets instead of the present forty-two, the implication was that – all things considered – they had tracked down the world of eternal life.

Its inhabitants had torn the whole planet from the gravitational pull of Vega but had left some clues. A curved line traversed the familiar constellation of stars. An examination had determined that this line was part of a far-flung elliptical orbit in which the roaming celestial body evidently moved. A very surprising fact had come to light. Mother Earth was precisely at one of the focal points of the ellipse. The coincidence suggested that the unknown taskmaster had chosen mankind for a special role.

The visitapes of the replica were studied in great detail, requiring complicated calculations, which they could never have attempted without the positronic computer on board the *Stardust*.

Now Perry Rhodan was on the threshold of the Unknown's abode, the being who was said to live longer than the sun. Providing the transition proceeded successfully!

This was the situation when the safety lock

clicked open. The large switch button was freely exposed in the armrest of the pilot seat.

Five seconds prior to the transition Rhodan released the so-called permit-impulse to the hyper-positronic brain controlling the transition. It was beyond human ability to influence, let alone to conduct such operations in hyper-space themselves.

Someone screamed – loud and shrill. Vega shot the searing points of its fiery protuberances almost into the deflection screen. They could no longer hear their own voices. The mighty *Stardust* had become a swinging bell.

It was as if they were bombarded by a rain of fire from an armada of battleships. Rhodan estimated the energy of a single medium-sized protuberance to be the equivalent of 1.2 million hydrogen bombs made on Earth.

Never before had the *Stardust* run into such an infernal holocaust.

During the last fraction of a second before the transition Rhodan noticed the violet outburst of the collapsing protective screens. All safety devices of the power-reactors blew simultaneously. They had reached the end of the line. The steely hull of the spaceship was helplessly exposed to the untrammeled forces of an exploding super-star.

Once more the shrill scream could be heard over the telecom. It pierced the deep rumbling until it faded into a faint whisper.

At this instant something had been created around the vessel which was no longer part of this universe. The Arkonide structure-field for the total reflection of four-dimensional forces had been formed just before the catastrophe. It converted the solid matter of the spaceship into a state of de-materialization during which it received the impulse for the transition.

The glowing metallic torch, which *Stardust II* was just now, vanished from normal space.

Rhodan carried that last cry with him in his de-materialized brain. The sound was still vivid in his senses as the spaceship returned into the normal universe after a short jump of eighty-three light-years. The transition had taken place – as usual – without any appreciable delay of time, although Arkonide science had proved that there was an-other factor present in the five-dimensional refer-ence system which could bear – for simplicity's sake – the connotation of time. According to this inter-pretation 123 years had just passed for the crew.

No changes had occurred in the normal space-continuum. The re-materialization followed only moments later on the ship's chronometer.

This time Rhodan had no trouble shaking off the last impressions before the hyper-jump. Neither had anybody else lost consciousness.

The encircling observation screens reflected the multitude of stars in the Galaxy. At the rear the videoscreens showed a particularly bright point.

It was huge Vega which glittered only with its usual light. The incandescent glow of the ex-plosion was not yet visible; eighty-three years would have to pass before the light could reach them here.

Rhodan wasted no time with superfluous conversation. He quickly checked the controls of the various engine units.

The programming for steering and supervising the automatic units, initiated before the transition, had obtained reactions swifter than any human being could think or act.

A deep rumbling made the *Stardust* vibrate again but this time it was caused by its own power sources. The engines had started up again with maximum output at the precise moment of re-emergence although no man was in a position to register it at the time.

The supership braked its speed at 300 miles per second, requiring the full resources of its power stations. If they failed when their capacity was exceeded, all men and material would be pulverized under the strain of the deceleration forces.

The thought of this peril was uppermost in Rhodan's mind. They were moving now as before almost with the speed of light and could slow down to zero within ten minutes – if the engines were in order.

Rhodan's hands began to work quickly. Bell looked up, muttering. He understood the score at once. The drone of the drive-engines rose above the sound of the power generators which also were required to furnish the current for the high-energy thrust-absorbers so vital for their safety.

Rhodan checked the power stations on the control screen. Some of the stupendous Arkonide reactors showed a violet light. They were out of order. Others were running properly but the bank of transformers lagged behind. All together they provided just enough energy for the neutralization projectors.

'Activate emergency switch!' the loudspeaker blared. 'Techno Control of positronic supervision recommends immediate reduction of extreme breaking rate. Energy supply running low. Advise caution.'

It was the mechanical voice of the robot-brain.

Bell lifted his hand. His fingers were over the central step-switch when he caught sight of Rhodan's eyes.

His facial expression was neither ironical nor humorous.

Rhodan's eyes were compelling unfathomable organs of command will power. Bell felt as if he were held in an iron grip. The irresistible hypnotic force in the gaze of his superior had never before been so starkly revealed.

'You won't do that, will you?' he heard Rhodan's calm voice through the muffled roar of the engines.

Bell's paralysis subsided. Grinning foolishly, he withdrew his hand from the switch.

'Of course not,' he said against his will. He recovered from his stupefaction when Rhodan's hypnotic eyes returned to normal.

Fascinated, Bell looked at the man whose inborn intelligence had been admirably schooled and reinforced by constant hypno-training. If Rhodan wanted something, there was no contradicting him, especially when he was emotionally involved in his demand. Even men of Reginald Bell's rank were reduced to helpless puppets.

The commander was already at work. He had no intention of delaying his rate of deceleration. Specific signals for counteracting the emergency were transmitted by direct impulse to the robot brain which executed and channeled the orders instantaneously.

In the hermetically sealed machinery halls, where no humans were present, special robots, comprising the widest variety, were put to work within seconds, repairing the damaged reactors.

When the automatic alarm sounded its whistle and the output was barely sufficient to supply the stress-absorbers, four large reactors began to function again.

Five minutes after the severe braking maneuver was initiated, the situation was once again under control. Now Rhodan took time for a second cup of coffee.

He looked slowly around at his aides in the command center.

The tip of Bell's tongue flicked across his lower lip. He watched Rhodan admiringly.

'You know,' Rhodan mused, 'we simply had to brake hard. Sure, some of the generators were knocked out. But if we had not cut back our lightning speed at the right moment and at the predetermined rate, we'd never be able to find the lost planet. We know its orbit and velocity. In about four minutes we'll have co-ordinated our movements. This will have to be done exactly at the point where the sunless planet is located in space. Can you imagine the mathematical problems we'd have to deal with if we had rushed by the computed point at high speed?'

Bell swallowed hard. 'I'd like to know what devil made me get on this spaceship,' he said disconsolately, squinting at his hand. 'I could have had a peaceful life and be a respected man in my little hometown. It's crazy what we're doing here, crazy!'

'Wait and see!' Rhodan counseled. 'Capt. Klein, take over the rangefinder section. The mutants are requested to attend a meeting in mess-hall 4 in five minutes. Thank you!'

Rhodan rose from his seat. The safety belt was again concealed in the backrest. He walked leisurely to the elevator and a hush settled over the command center after he was gone. Only Khrest murmured one sentence:

'He's destined to preside over the Great Imperium in the future.'

FOUR

DANGER IN DEEP SPACE

The Arkonide stereo-compensators were switched over to the large evaluation picture screen. Thus a precise co-ordination with the pictures taken was assured.

The adjusting maneuver had already required four hours ship time. It was an easy matter for the research cruiser and super-battleship, equipped with every conceivable instrument, to track down any existing planets in an uncharted solar system in space.

Their presence and accurate position were determined within a few minutes by the tele-sensors. It didn't take much more time to ascertain the information about mass, density, rotation, trajectory and velocity of the bodies.

In this particular case Rhodan had discarded from the outset any preconceived ideas and past experiences in familiar space. He was careful not to nurture any unjustified expectation.

The considerable time span of four hours necessary for the adaption to the computed orbit of the artificial planet Wanderer had already proved that unusual factors had to be taken into account.

The men on board the super-battleship tackled the extraordinary difficulties which were more challenging than all preceding missions.

The scanning operations continued for hours. A true picture of countless stars and distant isolated worlds glimmered and glistened on the screens. However, they were all too far away from the vicinity where they searched for the elusive body.

Rhodan joined the officer heading the computer section in the command center. The drive-engines were silent now after the final corrections had been made. The stereo-compensators indicated that *Stardust II* correctly followed the line of the ellipse around thirty-one suns along which the unknown planet moved.

The measurements were accurate to the tenth decimal. Nevertheless, variations of tolerances could have crept into the calculations, in fact could hardly be avoided considering the distances involved.

Khrest watched attentively the read-out and diagrams of the positronic computer. Evidently no mistakes had slipped in.

Thora stood stiffly and motionlessly in front of the array of instruments.

The most capable mutants of the special corps had assembled in the command center an hour ago.

They listened and applied their astounding and unique senses to get ahold of something nobody had ever seen or touched before and whose existence could only vaguely be comprehended.

Rhodan had called the object of their search Wanderer. Presumably this was a fitting definition for a celestial body returning once every two million years, terrestrial time, to the Vegan system unless it deviated from its course.

Pucky, the furry refugee from the planet Vagabond, cowered behind Rhodan on the floor. His shiny eyes longingly surveyed the many levers and switches. Rhodan's warning gesture made him gloomy and he bared his incisor. Obviously this was not the place to play games.

He sighed in disgust, rose ponderously and said with his squeaky voice:

'I'll go to the kitchen to see the cook. If you need me, Chief, tell John Marshall to call me.'

Rhodan watched the little fellow as he sauntered off. Pucky had the potential of becoming one of the most valuable additions to the corps.

Pucky stopped in front of the youngest member of the Mutant Corps. Betty Toufry was only ten years old but her psyche was not that of a mere child.

'Do you want to come with me?' Pucky asked. 'It's dull around here.'

The small face, framed by dark hair, broke into a radiant smile.

'May I?' Betty asked.

Anne Sloane, who was like a mother to the child on board the ship, saw that Rhodan nodded. She tried to be casual and cheerfully admonished them:

'Don't make any mischief! Don't throw the chef into the kitchenpots! I'll come and get you.'

Pucky's mood was cheered up in no time. He

60

had instinctively understood that there was only one person on the ship who was willing to play. He could only surmise the reason this came about. It seemed to have something to do with the age of the other people.

'We can let some frozen food fly down into the chef's collar,' Pucky suggested enthusiastically. 'The boss can't say that this endangers the security of the ship.'

Betty Toufry was now acting like a child again. She could change in seconds.

With playful ease the two accomplished telekinetic magicians opened the intricate electronic locks of the armored hatches. The hatches slid open, the switches remaining untouched.

'I was faster,' Pucky claimed. 'Do you want to fly?'

Reginald Bell silently followed the two dissimilar beings with his eyes. The wonderful accord between one of mankind's younger generation and the totally different denizen from the depth of the Galaxy was an encouraging sign. He had a vision of a harmonious world full of understanding and mutual respect.

It was the only way to build a commonwealth of the stars and to overcome the conflicts.

'The little ones are really compatible, aren't they?' Rhodan picked up Bell's train of thought.

The stout man flinched. He narrowed his eyes suspiciously:

'Since when are you telepathic? How do you know what I was thinking?'

'Reasonable men are likely to think of such things when they see a promising picture like this.'

'The chef will go mad.' Capt. Klein was worried. 'Yesterday they re-arranged everything in his re-frigerator locker.'

Rhodan didn't answer him. The little diversion had been pleasant but he had now other problems.

Behind a transparent partition sat the excellently trained radio-technicians of the battleship's range-finder section. They had learned by hypno-training.

Rhodan raised the micro-sender on his left wrist to his lips. His voice was heard, loud and clear, over the loudspeaker behind the partition.

'Deringhouse, did you get anything?'

A tall man, who could be seen sitting fifty yards away, turned his head. He could survey a part of the command center from his place.

'Nothing, sir,' his soft voice came over the minia-ture set. 'This space sector seems to be swept clean.'

'Didn't the mass-sensors register anything?'

'They show nothing at all. I'm bound to get an echo if there's something around within a light-month. There's only the usual micro-matter. A lonely atom once in a great while. A planet should be a little bigger than that.'

'Thank you for the lecture, Major,' Rhodan replied icily.

'I beg your pardon, sir. I forgot again that I have nerves.'

The final evaluation of the positronic brain came in. Rhodan leaned forward. The transition was successful, so was the co-ordinating operation and flight correction.

Slowly he reclined again. *Stardust II* was crawling at a ridiculous ten miles per second through space, which indeed appeared to be empty in this sector. Not even a measly meteor could be spotted by the best range-finder of all times, and they would have spotted it if it measured only one-thousandth of an inch.

It was a most unsatisfactory state of affairs. Rhodan slowly turned around and noticed Thora.

'A sour face, reproachful eyes and arrogant attitude in perfect combination, that's you,' Rhodan remarked facetiously.

'We could have been in Arkon by this time,' Thora said excitedly. 'But you won't listen, Perry! You'll never solve the last riddle, never! Take me and Khrest home at last as you have promised us long ago. Khrest doesn't insist on pursuing the secret of biological cell conservation. You have no right to risk our lives, Perry!'

'Aren't you forgetting the exploding Vega? Besides, our calculations are correct. The planet we're looking for is close by. Because it doesn't circle around a sun and emits no light of its own, we can't see it. But we have other means of detecting it.'

'You're heroic and dramatic!' the Arkonide woman mocked him. 'You'll probably detect nothing. Your calculations are inadequate. This planet could be a 100 light-years away, assuming of course that it exists at all which I doubt very much. You better turn back.'

Bell's wrinkled forehead hid his thoughts till he spoke up in a miffed tone:

'We're not turning back. I've a sinking sensation that somebody is leading us by the nose ad absurdum. I've got a good idea. Would you like to hear it, Perry?'

Rhodan sat down in a contour chair.

'If it's a good one we can talk about it.'

'The Unknown or, if you will, the Unknowns have played some rough games with us. It's only logical that every step we take becomes more difficult. Now we've the hardest nut of all to crack.'

'What else is new?'

'The planet is shielded from our direction finders, that's all. We ought to check out whether they function properly. Why don't you launch a small spacefighter and test how the instruments register the craft. That way we'll eliminate a very fundamental doubt.'

'That's an excellent idea,' Rhodan agreed after a pause. 'Major Nyssen ... !'

The shouted call went to all departments. Nyssen's craggy face appeared on the videoscreen.

'Here I am, sir!' he croaked. 'At my post in the hangar.'

'You don't say!' Rhodan snapped. 'Guess why I want you! Jump into your pursuitship. Blast-off in exactly five minutes, whether you're in your crate or not. Hurry up!'

Nyssen cursed horribly. They could still hear him after his craggy face had disappeared from the screen.

Marshall, the telepath, was aroused and disturbed.

'If you knew what he's thinking—!' he whispered. 'It makes me shudder.'

'Forget it,' Rhodan grinned. 'We've freedom of thought on this ship. Major Deringhouse!'

'Sir?'

The tall figure with the freckled face detached itself from its seat behind the transparent wall.

'You heard what we're planning to do. You won't believe it but Mr Reginald Bell had an idea. Switch on your range-finder three minutes after Nyssen has shoved off at full thrust. I want to see what your instruments will do. Nyssen, do you still hear me?'

Nyssen reported from the cockpit of his fighter. He had managed to climb into his machine within a few moments.

'You're free to fly anywhere. Choose your own course but make sure to watch your automatic direction finder all the time. Don't go any farther unless you keep the *Stardust* right on the sensor beam. You'd never find us again.'

'I've got air, water and food for a month,' Nyssen muttered. 'Okay, sir, I'll watch it.'

When the five minutes were up, the spaceship was slightly jolted. A fire-spitting phantom shot out of the gaping airlock above the bulging ring.

Nyssen's ultrafast single fightercraft zoomed into dark space. The glowing point was quickly out of sight.

'Nyssen to Commander,' the loudspeaker intoned. 'Automatic sensors work perfectly. *Stardust* is on beam. I won't lose you. Watch my dust! Over and out.'

Nyssen switched off the radio's microphone. The faster-than-light telecom took its place. Ordinary communication was no longer adequate.

His craft became an utterly forlorn speck groping in the endless depths of the universe. The *Stardust* was no longer visible. All Nyssen could hear was the droning of his impulse drive-engines. He hurtled at 300 miles per second into the void, leaving the mothership farther and farther behind. After three minutes ship time he cut off the power. The wild howling became a gentle hum.

The tiny pursuitship remained in free fall at 55,000 miles per second. Nyssen looked around. He already knew the feeling of unlimited loneliness. The missions in the Vegan system had probably been far more hazardous.

The thought gave him some comfort until he painfully realized that there was a little difference between the absolute void and a system crammed full of planets. There he could have landed anytime in an emergency, whereas here he had only the *Stardust* within reach. If it should vanish he would be lost forever.

Drops of sweat began to stand out on his forehead. He stared anxiously at the dial of the range-finder bathed in green light. The battleship was still clearly reflected as a blip.

Nyssen gripped the direction control lever of the energy impulse jet. Then he waited. The efficient range-finder of the *Stardust* should already have found him.

After another minute the seconds became suspenseful eternities. Finally, he jammed the lever for the field reversal into the notch while pulling the step-switch for the drive-engines all the way up with his left hand.

A violet glow shot forward from the braking jets of the needle-nosed fighter, checking his speed abruptly.

A weak noise was audible as his machine roared. The telecom clicked.

'Deringhouse to Nyssen. Return at once. Very urgent. Come back, do you hear me? Confirm order.'

Nyssen had a sinking feeling that something had gone awry. He shouted at the top of his voice that he got the message but the *Stardust* did not seem to hear him.

'Major Nyssen, confirm order! Return right away. Danger! Nyssen, report immediately!'

Thus the spacefighter pilot came to realize that his flight had precipitated a crisis. He slowly leaned back in his seat. His eyes searched for a tiny yellowish speck of light in the ocean of stars. One of these little points in the Galaxy was the terrestrial sun. Nyssen's thoughts began to blur. He vaguely felt that his life was coming to an end.

The engines of his pursuitship kept running.

FIVE

'YOU'RE OUT OF YOUR MIND'

'It wasn't such a good idea after all,' Bell fretted, as a sudden jerk tossed him to the floor where he remained to listen. Rhodan grabbed the armrests of the chair in front of the computer console.

The first shock was followed by a second, even more violent one. Nevertheless, all observation screens remained blank. There was nothing to indicate the possibility that an energy beam or anything similar had been aimed in their direction.

There was no sign of what could have caused the huge mass of the super-battleship to move, let alone set such violent vibrations into motion.

Next door Deringhouse shouted to get the spacefighter back that they had just launched. Nyssen's start had triggered something but nobody knew exactly what it was.

There was no panic on board the ship. They were accustomed to worse incidents since their first encounter with the puzzling antagonist in the Galaxy.

Rhodan put the microphone to his lips just as the fourth shock hit the spherical hull like a pressure wave.

'Commander to Energy Control Center!' His voice was heard in all departments. 'Please, keep calm! Garand, restore gravitational field, start with magnitude two. Check if the next shock hits with the same force.'

Capt. Klein had crawled to his weapons control center. The continuing vibrations prevented normal walking.

Garand reported back. The power reactors had started to hum again. He had lost no time in repairing the damaged installations and they now functioned properly just when they were needed.

The video screens began to light up with a faint blue. The strong gravity field surrounded the spaceship.

The vigorous shaking of the spaceship subsided immediately. Calm prevailed again with the return of self-stabilization.

Reginald Bell slowly lifted himself off the floor. Rhodan whistled softly and off-key. His gaze seemed to penetrate the walls.

'Hi, old friend!' he said as he raised his hand and began to wave.

Bell looked around everywhere. He couldn't see anybody where Rhodan waved.

He glanced imploringly at the physician on duty in the command center. It was Dr Eric Manoli who had been with them from the earliest days.

Manoli shrugged his shoulders and shook his head silently.

'I hope you feel alright,' Bell said solicitously. With a forced smile he gingerly approached his commander but he didn't get very close. Instead, he was bodily lifted up and not very gently deposited on his seat.

'Who did that?' he yelled, flushed with anger, to the group of mutants at the other end.

Tama Yokida, one of the Hiroshima mutants, raised his hand.

'I did,' he whispered. 'We have a rule against touching other people.'

Rhodan gave him a mildly disapproving look and got up.

Quiet had once more returned to the *Stardust*; but it was the quiet before a storm. Rhodan took his seat in front of the main control panel. Everybody watched him as he pressed the release for the safety harness. Seconds later the alarm began to wail.

The voice of the commander sounded calm. He did not think it necessary to make long explanations.

'Prepare for combat. Robot emergency commandos take their positions. Deringhouse, did you reach Nyssen?'

'He didn't call back,' Deringhouse answered in a disturbed tone.

'Keep trying. Does his ship show on your screen?'

'Yes, sir, the echoes are excellent. The instruments function perfectly.'

'That's what we wanted to find out. Attention, everybody! A force field is, to all appearances, interfering with us. Its nature is so far undefined. Be ready for surprises. You're advised to remain at

your battle stations for your own safety. Capt.
Klein, fire a random beam shot from the gun at the
upper pole. Deploy an impulse weapon. I want to
see the beam.'

'Shock waves are still coming,' reported the
energy control center. 'They're now absorbed by
the G-field.'

Bell had regained his composure.

'Who was that old friend you greeted?' he
quickly asked.

'Three guesses. Our mystery friend let us know
that he's around. I bet my bottom dollar we're near
the planet.'

'We ought to be able to see it or locate it with
the range-finder.'

Rhodan's face looked skeptical.

'We'll come to that too,' he predicted. 'The question is how.'

'Nyssen is gaining speed, he's giving it all he's
got,' Deringhouse announced. 'Shall I take over by
remote control?'

'By all means, hurry up. If I know the Unknown,
these shocks were only a little tidbit of his.'

Deringhouse switched on his guidance system.
Nyssen saw the red lamp light up above his head
and then he knew that the mothership had taken
him under its wings, regardless of whether his
signals got through or not.

Nyssen stared ahead with burning eyes. The climate control of his spacesuit turned itself on as
the humidity became excessive.

Finally, Rod Nyssen recognized the weak glimmer in the cluster of stars. The little flicker became more distinct until it disappeared again in the flames of his pursuitship. His flight was retarded by the *Stardust*. Next they would have to open the fatally dangerous gravitation screen to avoid a collision with the little fighter and to prevent its disintegration in a flash. It was always a test of nerves to approach the *Stardust* with enormous speed, knowing that it was enveloped in the most potent defense fields designed to repel all imaginable attacks.

Not that all types of defense screens were dangerous for materially stable objects but the G-field was one of those structures which incorporated the most lethal achievement of the Arkonide supertechnology.

It was, so to speak, abnormal in terms of three-dimensional space, since it consisted of energy-units of a higher order in the fifth dimension. The Arkonides knew the nature of gravity whereas the scientists on Earth had only tentative theories.

Nyssen's craft was still a fantastically fast projectile spewing redhot flames into black space.

The *Stardust* was still far ahead but clearly visible now. Seconds later it grew to the size of a baseball which stood out against the background of stars.

Nyssen's little machine gradually slowed down. He sighed hopefully and as he finally disengaged the manual steering, he saw with horror that one half of the battleship had suddenly become a fire-spitting furnace.

Nyssen managed to yell his observation into the telecom. Close before him the energy screen split open. Magnetic forces of enormous magnitude seized his craft and pulled it into the open hatch of the airlock.

It happened much too fast and rough. He kicked the pedal for the shock compensator almost at the instant that he was pushed onto the launching tracks with forbidding force and hurled into the magnetic retention field.

The little spacefighter slammed through the magnetic barrier and was smashed against the solid walls of Arkonide steel at the end of the hangar.

Before Nyssen lost consciousness he perceived the tumultuous uproar in the *Stardust*. After a long period of waiting things had perked up on the battleship.

* * *

It would have been too much to expect that Nyssen – in his condition – understood the reasons for his precarious landing maneuver. At present it was not so important how he got on board. What mattered was that he made it.

The two mutants in the command center, Son Okura and Tanaka Seiko, reacted almost simultaneously.

Okura, the frequency-seer, received only an in-

74

distinct wave pattern. Nevertheless, he was able to pinpoint the spot where the entirely unfamiliar emission originated.

It was located in the red sector at about thirty-two degrees. In the vertical plane it was at four degrees.

He reported his findings at once. However the other mutant, Tanaka Seiko, had suffered violent repercussions.

Anne Sloane and Tama Yokida restrained the frantic mutant by telekinetic force.

It was impossible to get accurate information. Tanaka's wretched condition had evidently been brought on by a severe shock.

It also quickly became superfluous to obtain the result of his directional probing. The *Stardust* had abruptly become the victim of overpowering forces.

Weeks of laborious calculations and intricate maneuvers were in danger of being negated within moments.

An unseen mailed fist struck at the same time as Nyssen's pursuitship landed in the airlock.

Rhodan had already switched over to automatic control when the first relatively mild strikes occurred. He feared that he would be in no position to counteract sudden surprises in time. The way it looked now, this seemed to have been a very appropriate move.

Stardust II was soon reduced to a creaking spherical shell whose cavernous volume was not conducive to retaining the necessary stability.

It was as if all joints and braces expanded and contracted although some reinforcements were armorplate a yard thick.

At the same time the spaceship's velocity increased spontaneously to such a degree that Rhodan's attention was primarily concentrated on listening to the power reactors instead of the distortion effects.

'Maximum load,' Bell shouted above the noise. Rhodan looked at the widened eyes of his friend. This was as much as Bell reacted to panic. He was one of those enviable men without nerves in times of danger.

The alarm went off again. Bright-red warning lamps blinked in all departments of the ship.

'Oh no, not this!' Khrest moaned as he was squashed in his seat.

Rhodan, too, could feel the mounting pressure. The mighty *Stardust II* was driven by ever-increasing accelerating forces with which the thrust neutralizers could cope no longer. Their capacity was 360 miles per second which could be exceeded in emergencies only for a very limited time if all power reactors worked together.

Rhodan began to look worried. Something was happening now which had not occurred on board a modern Arkonide spaceship in at least 20,000 years – the effect of the moment of inertia took over. They felt the impact of the thrust breaking without transition through the neutralizing field and they realized that the Unknown was deadly serious this time.

The automatic controls still functioned satis-factorily. So far only the men were hampered by the cruel forces.

Khrest's unusually young face became grotes-quely distorted. He suddenly looked ancient, dilapidated and lifeless. The Arkonide was almost unable to breathe while Rhodan still functioned and made decisions.

The more high-pitched sound of the drive-engines running at full speed insinuated itself into the predominant noise of the power reactors. The engines produced about four million tons of thrust by terrestrial standards.

Rhodan exhaled the compressed air in his lungs with a whistle. It felt like a sneeze of relief. He wanted to shout, laugh or do anything to vent his excitement.

He regained his lucidity. The engines performed in a faultless manner as was to be expected from the superior products of the Arkonides.

Brutal forces of formidable strength opposed each other. On one side the incredible energy of the Unknown and here the might of machines.

Bell stretched his limbs. Khrest and Thora were still unconscious and the physicians Haggard and Manoli rushed to their aid. The two Arkonides were the weakest persons on board. Even Pucky proved to be hardier.

'Absorbed, thank goodness,' Bell gasped. 'Oh, it's getting stronger again. We're losing the little bit of counter-thrust we gained against the repulsion radiation. Brother, it's going to be our neck this time.'

Bell grinned wryly. He no longer moved a finger. The faces of the officers appeared on the video-screens. The mutant Tanaka Seiko still raged violently in spite of the anesthetic administered by Dr Haggard. His extraordinary brain must have registered the unknown energy units with painful reaction.

Rhodan concentrated his thoughts. His mind was working feverishly. A vague concept began to form in his brain. The tachometer was going down to zero from the 1.5 miles per second headway they had made against the opposing force. They were nearing the end. The neutralizers became over-loaded.

Rhodan racked his brains. He ceased to hear the infernal noise around him. Then a revelation struck him like lightning.

'What did you say just now?' he shouted. Bell spun around as Rhodan gripped his shoulder.

'What is it? How did you call the field?'

'Field? I didn't say anything about a field. Do you mean repulsion radiation?'

Rhodan's reaction was not confined to a sigh of relief. His body surged across the instrument board up to the extreme right hand corner of the inclined panel where the main control of the energy screens was located.

His fist struck the lever. Foot-long sparks flashed

from the circuit-breakers as he shut off the current to the energy-screen projectors.

His men screamed in terror. Had their commander gone mad?

Bell was the first to grasp the meaning. The white-hot G-screen collapsed like a soap bubble blown away. It was as if its awesome power had never existed. The shrill howling of the generators and transformers died down. Only the drive-engines kept roaring at full capacity.

The *Stardust* – whose velocity had been so far incalculable – automatically reversed its direction at full speed and went where it had come from.

'Dammit!' Marshall exclaimed. 'It was our gravity field! They somehow used it as a pole to repulse us. Whatever made you think of that, sir?'

Rhodan laughed out loud. With undiminished attention he kept staring at the instrument panel. The mysterious interference had definitely been eliminated.

'Hello, old friend!' he called for the second time with a defiant grin on his lips. 'We won again! What comes next?'

This time Bell did not question Rhodan's sanity any more; he leaned back exhausted.

In the wide open space ahead of them the planet Wanderer followed its course through the Galaxy.

Khrest finally regained consciousness. He was appealing for help.

'It's all right now,' Rhodan said soothingly. 'Bell

mentioned something about a repulsion field which gave me the idea.'

'Repulsion radiation,' Bell corrected. 'Honestly, I don't know why, it just slipped out.'

'In that case let's have a little more slippage like that.'

Rhodan coughed. His lungs were still hurting.

'It was a little rough,' he commented. 'Be that as it may, the Unknown wields stupendous power. This has been the hardest test. Apparently he has no intention of surrendering his secret unless it is to somebody who knows how to safeguard it. I hope we don't weaken at the last moment.'

'Do you still dare to go on?' Thora cried, horrified.

Rhodan looked sternly at her.

'Vega is burning up, keep that in mind! Bell, take over the controls! I've got some work to do at the computer.'

'You're out of your mind, I'm sure of that,' Thora declared utterly amazed.

As the tall man walked past her with stooped shoulders, she glanced at him, bewildered and fascinated.

Klein winked at Bell who began to grimace and to whistle, a sure way to make Thora beat a hasty retreat.

'Stupid!' Thora put him down. 'You'll never learn, you ape! When we get to Arkon I'll have you put on the nearest tree.'

Tall and erect she swept past him to her seat. Bell stared at her flabbergasted.

Before Bell could let loose with his own pithy vernacular, the Unknown interrupted him again with a vengeance.

SIX

WORLD OF THE UNKNOWN

'Turn it off!' Rhodan bellowed, beside himself. 'Cut off the electric power for the protective screen! Shunt the current or short-circuit it. Do something! My controls are out of commission.'

'So are mine,' Garand replied cheerfully as if he were playing games with some children. However Garand's cheerfulness was a mask for deep concern. It was peculiar how much this man differed from most others.

Rhodan bit his tongue to suppress a derogatory epithet. Desperate and furious, he looked around:

'Any ideas, anybody? The engine controls are blocked. We've got to shut the engines off. If we don't brake within five minutes we're going to slam into something we can't even see.'

Khrest threw up his hands and returned to his seat in resignation. Klein nervously fingered his weapon controls and suggested:

'I could fire some Arkonide bombs or perhaps trigger gravity-bombs of the fifth dimension into the space-continuum. If there's anything ahead of us, it would be swept away.'

'Very smart,' Rhodan sneered. 'Your G-bombs are no faster than light and, therefore, no faster than we're moving. You'll have to think of something better than that. Who's got an idea? I can't think straight any more. Isn't there anybody else who can come up with an idea?'

Rhodan calmed down again. At first it seemed to have been only a trifling matter that had gone wrong with the *Stardust*.

With engines running at full speed the *Stardust* had in the meantime recovered the distance lost by the earlier repulsion. They had first come to a standstill and then shot forward again along the predetermined trajectory.

The engines had propelled the spaceship for about ten minutes when Khrest announced – after consulting the positronic brain – that it was time to slow down the craft in order to reach their previous position and velocity. Rhodan manipulated the controls in order to obtain a state of free fall and, subsequently, to brake their speed, but the racing engines failed to respond in a normal manner and continued completely out of control.

This was the situation they found themselves in. Something had jammed all controls. Apparently there was more to it than simple blocking. It drove Rhodan to desperation that he was unable to put his finger on it.

He looked around once more. None of his aides offered any advice, including those visible on the television screens.

A squeaky voice began to chirp behind the commander's seat. With a sudden intuition Rhodan swiveled around, grabbed Pucky firmly by the neck and jerked him forward. The furry animal yelped pitifully. The anger in his bright eyes waned as soon as Rhodan imploringly panted:

'Pucky, my little friend, now you can go into your first action. I'll let you play a little. Listen, you may play with all the engine controls the way you did once before. You know the big machinery hall where those red metal blocks are? They are the field-projectors for the protective screens. When they fail, the thermo-transformers and impulse converters are knocked out as well. Concentrate on the red metal blocks. Something is wrong with them. Stop the machines!'

'I know, I know!' Pucky exclaimed, bubbling over in exhilaration. 'I've played with those back home. Did I get a bang out of them!'

'Go ahead! Let it rip!'

The mutants excitedly watched the most accomplished telekinetic being of all times. Not even little Betty Toufry had such faculties at her command. Betty jumped up and offered her hand to Pucky. His tiny paw disappeared in her hand.

'Will you help me? Please, come with me, but let me do it, just support me!'

Rhodan kept a watchful eye on the videoscreen showing the power-transformer station in the machinery hall. It was an attempt fraught with danger which, however, could very well be crowned with success.

The yowl of the engines continued unabatedly for a while until they began to sputter. A shower

84

of sparks streaked from the transformer shields. A terrible crash made the *Stardust* quiver.

Suddenly it was all over. The engines were silent and the bright glow of the impulse currents disappeared from the observation screen.

Betty Toufry collapsed without a sound. Anne Sloane picked her up and bedded her down on a contour couch. Pucky rested his furry head on Klein's knee. He was trembling all over and moaning softly.

'Well done, shorty, you were great!' Capt. Klein stammered, stroking the silky fur. 'Everything is going to be just fine.'

Rhodan began to operate his switches. He did not know which connections the two telekinetics had broken with their extraordinary psychic power. In any case, all installations functioned properly. However, the automatic navigation control was a few seconds late when it warned:

'Emergency! Garand, prepare for energy requirements at 350 miles per second.'

This time all orders were quickly executed. The force field was automatically restored in an exemplary manner.

Minutes later the high velocity of the vessel was reduced to practically nil.

Then Tanaka Seiko began to have another fit of violent madness. He drew himself up despite his drugged state, stared ahead with frightened eyes and screamed incoherently, although there was nothing to see on the observation screens except empty space. The range-finder did not register anything either.

Rhodan activated the override emergency switch. The hatches slammed shut and the magnetic harnesses popped out to hold the men securely in their seats.

At this moment a terrible crash shook the entire spaceship. Notwithstanding that the absorbers were operating at full strength, they were shoved forward into their safety harnesses. The belts cut into their bodies with excruciating pain. Instruments clattered and broke into thousands of pieces in the aftermath of a fifty-G shock which burst without restraint through the absorber field.

A harrowing picture began to unfold on the observation screen. The mighty *Stardust* had come to a grinding halt in an instant. The engines continued to run and shed some light on a half energy, half material substance which arched far and wide in all directions.

Rhodan stopped the engines. The more sensitive instruments had been shattered under the impact. The intercom was greatly impaired.

The gigantic sphere of the super-battleship had bored itself into a resilient object which it had hit with incredible force.

When Rhodan came out of his initial shock he grimly surveyed the situation and muttered:

'This landing wasn't exactly according to the book. Unusually messy, I'd say. What next? What are we up against now?'

86

He didn't have long to wait for an answer. A sun lit up, becoming brighter and brighter until it blinded their eyes.

It revealed far below a landscape which looked unreal. They had not landed on its surface but were suspended way up in a transparent dome. The *Stardust* had been stopped like a bullet in an impenetrable barrier.

Then they heard an uproarious Homeric laughter. Somebody howled with such pleasure that it threatened to split their ears, although they listened to it subconsciously. Evidently it was a telepathic feat of most impressive proportions.

'Hello, old friend,' Rhodan said for the third time. 'We've arrived, haven't we?'

The laughter ended as abruptly as it had begun. *Stardust II* started to descend. It fell faster and faster.

When they noticed the first noise of friction, doubtlessly indicating an atmosphere, the anti-grav field was activated.

After a short counter-thrust from the engines the spaceship was brought to a standstill five miles above the land.

They were enthralled by the sight on the observation screens. What they beheld was anything but a normal planet of the usual spherical shape with flattened poles.

What they confronted looked like a monumental agglomeration of strange architecture running the gamut from creations of genius to ugliness. The

Unknown had built a world to suit his own imagination.

It was awesome and fantastic, confusing and reassuring at the same time. If this was the world of eternal life, it was aptly designed and named.

'Great Scot!' Rhodan said deeply moved, 'I didn't expect anything like this. This is only a flat horizonless disk covered with oceans, forests, mountains and prairies; a circular slab topped and screened by a dome of energy. If one approaches it from below, nothing can be seen of this immense slab without light and vegetation; just an oversize slab. It's a world whose end can always be reached since it lacks curvature. Then you face the energy screen behind which empty space begins. It's simply a round platform with a roof. Have I lost my mind or have we all died?'

He turned his head. His men looked white as sheets. Pucky was still whimpering. The Unknown had stopped laughing.

SEVEN

THE MONSTER FROM NOWHERE

Approximately two minutes after passing through the most forbidding energy screen they had ever encountered, the hitherto transparent wall began to get clouded.

First it looked like muddy water, then milk, and finally opaque and solid. By the time Rhodan decided on a flight to explore the weird world, a part of the odd 'sky' had turned black and numerous stars twinkled in it. None of the constellations looked familiar. The display of stars on the inside of the energy dome far above the spaceship was completely different from anything in the Milky Way. It was an alien galaxy which could provide the first conjecture as to where *he* had come from.

The Unknown was now simply referred to as *he*. *He* had created an artificial private world on a slice of land which paralleled some of the outdated theories of the ancient scientists on Earth, when they still believed that the Earth was a flat disk floating on water with a heaven above.

One of the first inquiries Rhodan made concerned the interesting possibility that there could be a connection between the artificial representations of this world and the earliest concepts of earthbound astronomy. He was led to believe that such a connection might exist by the fact that one of the focal points of the elliptical orbit traced by Wanderer coincided exactly with Terra. He programmed the positronic brain for this question although he was not very sure that it could be answered.

While the positronic computer tackled the problem, the crew of *Stardust II* faced another more serious dilemma.

The spaceship was suspended in the neutralizing anti-grav field five miles above the ground. The eerie landscape posed numerous puzzles. Its mere existence was weighing heavily on their minds.

Rhodan returned to his pilot seat with the evaluation read-out from the computer. *Stardust II* was ready for battle action. Every man was at his station. A briefing over telecom had been called five minutes ago.

As Rhodan opened the briefing his face appeared in all departments on the screen. His voice was calm and sharply accentuated.

'This is your commander speaking,' Rhodan stated the obvious. Bell noticed that Rhodan chose to speak formally. He was every inch the all-demanding authority.

'It has been confirmed that the data for our transition from Vega to our present position have been correctly calculated. This world is exclusively of artificial nature. Machines are providing everything – from necessary heat to keeping it on course – which occurs naturally on other planets. We've to understand that whatever unusual happens here, is done intentionally and cannot be considered normal.'

He glanced quickly at his notes.

'The artificial planet Wanderer can be described as a gigantic and completely self-sufficient space station. It consists of a sheet of land 350 miles thick on the average. The density is high, natural minerals are abundant. It must be assumed that the ground was formed from collected micro-matter. Therefore, it has been created in the same basic manner as natural planets developed. Please don't ask me how *he* did it. The ground disk is very large; it measures close to 5,000 miles in dia-meter and we have thus a considerable mass of land there below studded with mountains and oceans. The atmosphere is enclosed in the energy dome and the climate is regulated. The prevailing gravity is pegged at 0.9 G and is apparently mechanically produced although the very heavy mass of land is contributing its gravity. A world has been estab-lished here which consumes terrific amounts of energy from tremendous power sources. We've previously discovered that this planet circled Vega 10,000 years ago. Then it vanished from the system just as we left it in our little spaceship. Quite re-markable, I admit.'

Rhodan listened with a faint smile to the audible breathing of his men.

'Remarkable, indeed! The atmosphere inside the air-tight energy dome is fit for us to breathe. It is clear that someone possessing incomparable technical resources has built a world where *he* assembled everything he deemed beautiful, desirable or interesting. Don't jump to the conclusion that we've found God himself at work. We're merely face to face with a living being whose technology, science and culture must be millions of years old. *He* has learned all the laws of nature by scientific methods. What looks like miracles are no more than very intricate phenomena engineered with the help of machines. Don't let it mislead you!'

Rhodan paused for a moment.

'It is obvious that we could not have entered this artificial world through the energy dome against *his* will. That *he* has admitted us proves that we've passed all tests to his satisfaction. Now we've reached *his* private realm. Remember the mad laughter which greeted us by telepathy. Compared to *his* knowledge the Arkonides are helpless dilettantes just as men from the stone age appear to us today. Keep that in mind and trust *his* good will. Don't take it for granted that we've persevered through all our tribulations by our initiative alone. *He* has always exerted restraint as soon as *he* found that we managed to parry *his* attacks temporarily. A candidate should never be tested beyond his endurance. One can take him to the brink, but that's where it has to stop. This is what has happened to us. Therefore, the situation looks very favorable in principle. This is the place whose inhabitants know the secret of biological cell conservation according to ancient traditions. If you have any doubt about it, think of the incredible events which have brought us here. Whoever can perform such momentous deeds must know a great deal about the mysteries of organic life. The old tales proved to be true even though reality shows differences in important respects. Here is somebody who is willing to recognize us from now on. Major Deringhouse ... !'

Deringhouse snapped to attention.

'Your request for a reconnaissance flight in fighter crafts is denied. Only on board the *Stardust* can we stay reasonably secure. The crew remains at battle stations. I'm afraid that we'll get a few more surprises. That's all. Thank you!'

Rhodan signed off. He preferred not to take part in the lively discussions between his men.

Minutes later the super-battleship started to move again. Proceeding at the slow speed of 900 miles per hour the *Stardust* traveled under the strange 'sky' where a yellow-white sun burned, guided by unseen forces.

Although they flew at an altitude of only five miles, they had an almost perfect panoramic view. Due to the lack of curvature the flat surface did not have a horizon in the customary sense. The view was only restricted by large objects in the line of sight.

Khrest was busy preparing a simple 2-D map. The geographical recording instrument operated continuously. The light-reflexes of the sensor-impulses scanning the landscape recorded all topographical features instantaneously.

The impulses bounced back from the faraway walls of the energy dome rising precipitously into the 'sky.' The resulting measurements were highly accurate.

Rhodan sat in his pilot seat and leaned forward. The large observation screens depicted fascinating details all around the ship.

The Mutant Corps clustered around Rhodan's seat. Since the spaceship had penetrated the wall of energy Tanaka Seiko had stopped raving and fallen asleep from exhaustion.

'Do you notice anything?' Rhodan asked without turning his head. John Marshall, Betty Toufry and Ishy Matsu were uncertain and answered in the negative until the little girl timidly said:

'Perhaps a teeny whispering, sir, but I can't make it out. How many people are supposed to be present here? Do they think clearly?'

Rhodan smiled. 'My child, I wish I could tell you that; but whoever is out there, *he* is thinking more than clearly.'

'*He?*' Betty repeated softly with a distant look in her big dark eyes. 'Couldn't there be more than one or is that a silly question?'

'Of course not. You may be on to something. Do you mean that there are many persons out there?'

'It does sound like it. The whispering is so curious. It is as if millions of people were talking to

94

each other.'

Reginald Bell became disturbed. Unsure of himself, he looked around at the mutants.

'I'm getting a creepy feeling,' he confessed with an embarrassed grin. 'What the devil is going on here? Nothing seems to be tangible and real. The landscaped park down there looks like something out of Old England. John, can't you recognize any thought impulses at all?'

Marshall's thin face twitched under the mental strain. Breathing heavily, he gave up his efforts.

'It's useless, there are no identifiable impulses coming through. If there is anybody, he must be immune to telepathic influence. All I can hear is a faint meaningless whispering.'

The dainty Japanese girl Ishy Matsu nodded eagerly.

'He's right,' she agreed, 'I can't make any contact either.'

Rhodan refrained from commenting. His uneasy feeling grew by the second.

High mountains rose up in the distance.

'For heaven's sake – it's snow!' Nyssen, who was busy at the sensor, announced after the analysis. 'Snow, imagine that! The highest peak reaches 23,000 feet. How did *he* do it?'

'And no people around anywhere. A world of splendor, completely abandoned,' Bell mused.

They flew over the snowcapped mountains. Deep down in the valleys, primeval tropical forests grew luxuriantly. Close by, sheer mountains of rocks rose high up into the air. The gorgeous scenery showed the flair of having been created in an inspired frenzy. In any case, the technical effort required boggled the mind.

A superior intelligence had skilfully used all natural forces. The flora from every part of the Galaxy had been collected. There were so many different species on display that they must have originated on numerous celestial bodies with highly diversified climatic conditions.

Wanderer seemed to house a conglomeration of all varieties. When they encountered the first flying creatures, they proved to have as many contrasting features as the profusely sprouting vegetation.

Prehistoric giants weaved through the air with slowly flapping wings and huge opened beaks ready to fight. They must have come from a planet in the early stage of development such as Venus where similar flying giant lizards roamed.

Nearby, fine-feathered birds were seen on the magnifying screen. They were unlike anything they had seen before. The birds were chased by snakelike animals with four wings.

Their eyes feasted on an endless variety of animals. It was a truly magnificent zoo where the most beautiful and interesting selections from the animal kingdom had been carefully gathered from the other planets; a presentation of wildlife in a multitude of forms.

The mountains came to an unexpected end when an ocean appeared. Rhodan did not trust his eyes when the *Stardust* suddenly flew over a dense bank of clouds. The sensor observation revealed far below a storm-tossed sea which was whipped into foam by the gales of a hurricane.

'I'm going to flip my mind!' Bell said tonelessly. 'Just look at that ahead of us! We're approaching an antediluvian forest the likes of which doesn't even exist on Venus. This is a real jungle, man!'

Rhodan stifled an expression of awe. It had become very quiet on board the spaceship. The men sat enchanted before the picture screens.

The hurricane raged only over the ocean and ceased where the jungle began as abruptly as it had started. Now the telesensors registered steamy hot-house temperatures. Wide swamps came into view where multicolored flowers in all hues were struggling for the light of the artificial sun.

'Beautiful, breathtakingly beautiful!' Anne Sloane whispered. 'Whoever has planned this must have been a botanist, zoologist, engineer and many other things all rolled into one. How much imagination and time must have been expended to bring all these plants and animals together! It's impossible that it could have developed completely naturally.'

'That's out of the question,' Rhodan agreed, overwhelmed by his feelings and thoughts. 'It couldn't have been done, Anne. First the extensive ground-plate was established. Then countless planets were searched by ultrafast spaceships and everything which struck *his* fancy was imported.

This must have been created by the whim of one individual, a truly cosmic master builder. Come to think of it, it has not been *created*, it has been built. There's a difference, I believe ...'

At this point, Anne screamed hysterically as something shook the ship and maddened cries pierced the telecom simultaneously.

Rhodan swiveled around in his chair. A gargantuan monster had appeared without warning in the range-finder section behind the adjacent transparent partition. Deringhouse was fleeing frantically. The radar technicians jumped from their seats to escape the flailing tentacles of the abominable beast.

The monster was a slimy steaming mass with a round body exceeding thirty feet. It was goggle-eyed and its sharp birdlike beak was snapped wide open. Its tentacles swung wildly around in all directions and when they touched an object it was roughly torn from its mountings and pressed into the jelly-like mass of its body, where it disappeared.

With the screaming of the men in his ears, Rhodan rushed toward the open hatch of the range-finder section.

'Matter-transmitter,' someone shouted. '*He* put the rotten beast right in our laps!'

As Deringhouse pulled his weapon from the holster, the atrocious monster became airborne. Rhodan smelled the all-pervading stench while the animal ascended and smacked against the domed ceiling with a loud splash; there it remained.

'Good work, Pucky!' Rhodan muttered, raising his impulse-beamer. He sprayed the hissing thermo-beam all over the writhing body, ravaging it severely.

Bell appeared on the scene with a heavy disintegrator, vaporized the ugly mass and finished it off, but not without dissolving part of the ceiling.

It took only a few moments, then the last remnants of the repulsive creature fell down and cracked some more good equipment.

Coughing strenuously, all men retreated from behind the transparent wall and Betty Toufry let the hatch slam shut. The automatic climate control began to suck out the corrosive gasses and vapors. The ceiling still glowed dark red; Rhodan's blast had hit not only the beast.

Deringhouse coughed spasmodically and doubled up with pain. He looked pale and glanced at his seat where he had been on duty a little while ago.

'Silence on board!' Rhodan bellowed into the telecom. 'It's all over. I've told you that we must expect surprises. I'm sure that the beast was transported into the ship by a matter-transmitter. Klein, take the robot work detail and have the department cleaned up.'

One of the radar technicians groaned and collapsed. Under the torn sleeve of his uniform the flesh of his arm was blistered. Rhodan rushed to his aid and called Haggard who waded through the group of men with their weapons ready to shoot.

'He got too close to the beak of the beast,' another man said hastily. 'I saw it happen. I wonder whether it was poisonous?'

Dr Haggard examined the wound quickly and thoroughly. His face showed an expression of deep concern.

'Help me. I've got to take him to the sickbay at once. I don't know yet what's wrong with him.'

Two men carried the casualty to the main elevator. In the room next door fast-working robots removed the remains of the monster under the direction of the positronic brain.

Rhodan went to get a drink from the dispenser. He silently listened to the excited discussions going on among the crew. They had been sorely tried. The fun and games are getting a little too rough, he thought.

'What's the matter?' Bell inquired.

'Nothing. How does it look on the land?'

Before Bell could answer, a report came from the upper pole cupola. They had discovered the towering buildings of a big city which was still about 1,800 miles away.

Rhodan inspected the navigation control room. The corrosive fumes had been sucked out; clean air was circulated by the blowers. The men cautiously returned to their posts and surveyed the destruction wrought by the monster.

Deringhouse fussed and cussed horribly. Finally he turned to Khrest and grumbled:

'I'd like to know where the thing came from. Khrest, have you ever seen such an animal? It was a veritable mountain of jelly.'

The Arkonide scientist shook his head. Ever since they had penetrated the energy cover, he had been very quiet. Only his reddish eyes were shining.

This was the world he had set out to find many years ago. He had finally arrived at the goal of his fondest desire. He had high hopes that his body, and hence his brain, could be perpetuated here forever. Because of the general decline in the Great Imperium a clear and active mind was bitterly needed to have among the leading members of the High Council. Khrest watched the observation screen attentively. He was the representative of a race in an irreversible process of degeneration after 20,000 years of conquest in space and building a glorious empire of stars.

He, Khrest, was entitled to receive the benefit of the coveted biological cell conservation!

EIGHT

INTER-CENTURY SHOOT-OUT

The city seen below was situated on a wide plateau on the banks of a broad river which rushed down over a rocky precipice into a deep blue ocean not far from the outskirts of the city, making Niagara Falls looks like a fine trickle by comparison. The rugged craggy rocks had been washed out by the tumbling torrents of water. The worn and polished stones were obviously a result of the water's action and gave no appearance of artificial arrangement.

Nothing could have demonstrated more conclusively that this artificial planet must have dated back to very ancient times, probably older than mankind and Earth itself.

The masses of water spilled down 2,500 feet. At the other shore of the 600-mile-wide sea they detected another settlement. The magniscreen had disclosed wooden sailing ships with horny-skinned two-legged beings on board.

When Rhodan descended with the *Stardust* to take a closer look at the dazzling city, nobody there paid any attention to the gigantic spacesphere. The unfamiliar inhabitants seemed to pursue their normal activities.

Then Rhodan moved to the south of the widespread city where prairies stretched out. The events they were about to witness stirred the visitors very deeply.

It was undeniable that the landscape exhibited the same contours as the Black Hills of South Dakota. Even more remarkable was the sight of red Indians fighting a bloody skirmish with bearded white-skins. The deafening noise of shots from big caliber guns was picked up by the sensitive microphones.

It was simply too much. Rhodan landed near the scene of the wild battle. An officer in a dark blue cavalry uniform came galloping toward the *Stardust* swinging his saber. He rode a magnificent stallion and Rhodan was surprised to find himself looking into the barrel of an 1867 Colt.

A sudden blast from Bell, who lost his nerve, made the apparition vanish. It had been an illusion. The magic was so lifelike and impressive that the men of the landing commando turned pale and remained shaken for some time.

They were about to leave again, thoroughly convinced that the people aboard the sailing ship were nothing but hallucinations either, when Lt Everson decided to walk over to the place where the cavalry officer had ridden through the prairie. Lt Everson suddenly screamed like a madman. He had found something in the high grass which was very real indeed.

Rhodan and the *Stardust* took off again in considerable haste.

Now he was contemplating – in a little room

close to the command center – the object found by Everson in the grass. It was lying in front of him on a little table beside his cup of steaming coffee.

It was a genuine Colt revolver, called Peace Maker, from the year 1867. The perfectly preserved, spotless weapon was loaded with six .45 caliber bullets. The ammunition with blunt points of soft lead was notched crosswise to cause severe damage to the victim. The barrel was six inches long. An examination of the material indicated that it had been manufactured during the latter half of the 19th century with the fabrication methods of that time.

Everson sat at the opposite end of the table. With a wan face he looked as if spellbound at the weapon.

'My dad had one of these,' he mumbled. 'For heaven's sake, where did this old gun come from? It's sheer madness; I'm going to lose my mind. If it was only a vision, why was this authentic gun lying in the grass? I know the model very well, sir. I've used it myself many times. This is the real thing, not an imitation. Just look at the ejector.'

Rhodan relaxed a little. It was obvious that Everson's nerves were shot. The commander thought for a moment. Then he removed the bullets from the six-shooter.

'Winchester - ammunition,' Everson hastily pointed out. 'Believe me, sir, it's the original thing!'

'Very well,' Rhodan finally said, 'but not very important.' He looked slowly around at the men standing in a circle around them.

'You must have realized by now that we're undergoing a final test. This,' he pointed to the Colt, 'is part of a war of nerves. You can see for yourselves what it did to Everson whose nerves could never be ruffled before. The origin of the weapon doesn't matter. Klein, have you asked the men whether anyone carried such a gun as a hobby?'

'Nobody, sir,' Klein assured him.

'Okay, so *he* has exercised another one of the incredible means at his disposal. *He* has replayed Custer's Last Stand before our eyes just as it must have really happened. Who knows, maybe those fighters locked in battle were transposed for a few short seconds to another plane in time? I'm afraid the historians will never be able to verify it. In any case, the Colt is here and it was recently fired. Don't let it throw you! We're now playing for keeps and we must have steady nerves.'

'But the gun was lying in the grass,' Everson repeated softly.

'Of course it was there. You know very well that *he* can travel in time, too. We've experienced it ourselves previously. Somehow he got that six-shooter out of the past from Earth. Don't let it worry you. I don't get it either how *he* did it. All I can tell you is that *he* knows everything about us on Earth. How else could *he* be so sure that our emotions would be so deeply affected by Custer's infamous struggle with the Sioux? *His* intention is to provoke us. Doesn't it dawn on you yet, Ever-son?'

The husky officer had a pensive expression in his eyes.

'I'll wring *his* neck,' he growled. '*He* nearly drove me crazy.'

Rhodan smiled and stuck the weapon under the belt of his uniform.

'You don't mind, Everson? There are only six bullets but you can have some made, if you like.'

Rhodan saluted casually. He dropped the matter when he saw that his men had begun to relax again.

Ten minutes later the super-battleship set down for the second time on the surface of this artificial world. It landed on a circular site, measuring one and a half miles in diameter, which was big enough to accommodate the *Stardust*, standing on its tele-scoped legs and rising to the imposing height of 2,500 feet.

The mighty spaceship was overshadowed by a tower at the edge of the field which exceeded its height by more than 1,500 feet. Looking slim and fragile, it pointed toward the energy dome which from this distance gave the appearance of a true, radiant blue sky with lovely little clouds.

The engines were shut off after the long flight. Outside everything looked quiet and serene. Neither animals nor humanoids could be seen.

The scene was still and peaceful but too lifeless for comfort. The faint, all-pervasive hum was easily disregarded. It seemed to be part and parcel of this world of technical wonders.

Rhodan remained a few more moments in his seat and scrutinized the surroundings. His optical instruments rendered a clear, colorful and brilliant picture.

The spacious plaza seemed to be the center of an industrial city. What were probably the most important buildings had been erected here by the city planner.

Smooth and unbroken metal structures of bold design dotted the ground which also had a metallic sheen.

The preponderant architecture was manifested in domed buildings with cantilevered protrusions but there also were rectangular constructions and cylindrical shapes.

The overall effect was harmonious and well-balanced.

Rhodan felt tired. He took off his radio helmet and replaced it with a cap. He sighed a little as he swiveled around in his chair.

The men were at their stations in the command center. Not a word could be heard over the telecom.

'The end of a great journey,' Rhodan said softly. 'Somebody is awaiting us. I wonder if we'll ever know who it is that lives longer than the sun. Well, Khrest, you have finally come to the fulfillment of your dreams. Let's go outside, or are you still afraid?'

The Arkonide was decked out in the costume of

his native world. His loose violet robe displayed the vivid symbols of the ruling Arkonide dynasty over his chest.

'I'm ready, thank you,' Khrest replied with dignified poise. 'Aren't you going to accompany me?'

Rhodan reluctantly got up from his seat. Tall, haggard and unshaved, in a slightly soiled uniform, he stood before the representative of a race to which mankind owed a great deal. This much was certain: if Khrest on his search for this artificial world had not crash-landed on the terrestrial Luna, mankind would most likely have had to wait a few more centuries for the beginning of space travel at speeds faster than light.

Rhodan was not one of those who would forget small or great favors. Slowly, he brushed his sweat-soaked hair from his forehead. With a mischievous look in his eyes, he growled:

'You boys look like a gang of highway robbers. When was the last time you cleaned up? I can't remember having seen a neat shirt since we left Ferrol.'

Bell wiped his hands on his pants in disgust.

'I preferred to keep my weapons clean,' he grumbled. 'When did we have time to take a bath during the constant turmoil?'

'You're hardly a conspicuous exception, Reginald,' Thora interjected sardonically. 'Well-bred Arkonides always use deodorant micro-filters in the presence of underdeveloped barbarians.'

Bell grew apoplectic with rage. Rhodan winked at the alluring woman and something began to happen to Thora which nobody had experienced before. She broke out in rollicking laughter.

Bell shut up in the middle of a word. His eyes seemed to pop out of their sockets.

'This takes the cake,' he moaned, defeated. 'It's unbelievable – the stuck-up dame can laugh!'

Rhodan gained the impression that Thora had just now freed herself of the haughty arrogance with which she was brought up. He couldn't take his eyes off her and kept stroking his stubbly beard with the back of his hand. The cap with the emblem of the New Power sat cocked and crumpled on his head.

'Okay, break it up!' he declared. 'Bell, summon the landing commando! Marshall, Pucky, you're coming too. The other mutants will take the second car. Major Nyssen, take over the command of *Stardust II* during my absence. Don't try to take off if anything unforeseen should happen. You'd never make it out to free space. The battle alert continues to be in effect. Stay on the ball and don't get any hare-brained ideas! Any questions?'

Rhodan got no questions. Bell left with a furious look at Thora. Tall and erect, clothed in the immaculate snow-white uniform of a super-battleship commander, she took her place next to the scientific leader of her shipwrecked research expedition. Her violet cape was a sign that she also belonged to the ruling dynasty on Arkon.

Down at the bottom of the vessel the airlocks were opened up. Feet trotting over long gangways could be heard. The landing commando consisted of twenty selected men under Rhodan's personal leadership.

* * *

Bell, who was driving the first car, stopped suddenly. The three other multi-purpose vehicles did likewise.

Speechless, the men stared ahead from the opened top-hatches of their vehicles. The air was mild and pure and the atomic sun shone benignly.

However, it was something else again which made Reginald Bell swear loudly.

It's rather unusual to serve a rotten tomato on a golden plate but it was much more unusual to see a grimy cowboy appear out of nowhere and begin to cavort wildly in front of the vehicles, all the time spitting on the ground.

Rhodan's face broke out in a broad grin. It was about time they had a little fun. Of course, this was just another phantom created by the Unknown. There could not be any other possible explanation. Evidently, *he* relished the sight of the perplexed visitors from Earth and enjoyed driving them to despair.

Rhodan warily got out of the car. The westerner spat out again, exposing the blackened stumps of teeth in his puffed up face. He had his thumbs stuck in his ammunition belt and two heavy .45

caliber Colts dangling in his holsters. Clad in dirty leather pants and cowboy boots with big spurs, he was the typical personification of an outlaw from the Old West just as the men had seen them in the movies.

He seemed to have a sense of humor. Apparently, *he* believed that the crew of the spaceship could be thoroughly impressed by the characters of the Old West. In this *he* clearly succeeded. Rhodan alone reacted in a contrary manner.

He advanced toward the figure standing in his way with his feet planted wide apart. Bright-red hair sprouted from his open shirt collar.

Rhodan was startled when the hitherto expressionless face became animated.

'Hi, pardner,' the individual rasped with a western dialect. 'What are you up to? If you make a false move, I'm going to pump you full of lead. Got it?'

Rhodan was taken aback. He silently watched the reckless desperado who spat again, this time hitting the tip of Rhodan's shoe. Rhodan managed to control his annoyance.

Bell hollered something and Rhodan was flat on the ground. A blast roared from Bell's impulse-beamer and enveloped the gunman in fiery flames. When the flash of fire was over, the gunslinger was still there, chuckling and taunting them spitefully:

'That's what you think, man! I'm for real. It's either you or me. I'll be damned if I know what's going on here but I've been told that I can't be plugged by you except in my time. Do you understand that?'

Rhodan got up. His face remained impassive.

'Drive on!' he ordered curtly. Then he turned around.

Two shots rang out almost simultaneously. Something hit the metallic ground, barely missing Rhodan's feet. The flattened bullets ricocheted and continued with a whistling sound.

Rhodan stopped in his tracks. Bell shot again, using the deadly disintegrator. The target just kept making faces.

'Only in my time,' he repeated. 'It's you or me, brother. That's what they said. I'm a damn good shot. You've got to be pretty fast to beat me to the draw. I don't mind telling you that you must head for that red gate over there but I've got the key in my pocket. If you can't bamboozle me out of it within the next half hour, I can go back and you can go to hell. Those scoundrels have told me that I was already dead, laid low by some lousy sheriff. I wouldn't doubt it! I've got two holes in my belly to prove it.'

He tore his filthy shirt open. Rhodan felt weak in the knees when he observed the two bullet-sized holes with dried blood in the apparition. What in the world had *he* conjured up!

The mutants back in the vehicles were making contact with the stranger.

'He's alive!' Marshall shouted excitedly. 'Be

careful, he's really alive!'

Pucky stood up on his seat. He tried but was unable to move their opponent telekinetically since he was apparently well protected from any and all influences.

'We've reached an impasse,' Khrest resignedly said in a muted tone. 'This is the final test. It's a living being. He emerged from another time plane and he is safe-guarded against all attacks.'

Rhodan studied the spot where the shots had made their impact. It left little doubt that two leaded bullets had hit the hard metallic ground.

'Twenty minutes to go and your time will be up,' the grubby stranger warned. 'They told me that I'll live again. Do you understand that, pardner?'

Rhodan hurried back to the vehicle. On his orders the vehicles started to race toward the red gate. It was a high, asymmetrically formed portal which was protected by a field of energy shimmering reddishly.

Bell pulled up to a sudden stop. When Rhodan got out of the car, the gunman appeared again.

'It's no use,' he scoffed. 'You sure got a funny looking wagon there!'

Rhodan's mutants tried all the tricks in their repertoire to no avail. They were up against an unassailable, supernatural power beyond their reach. Nothing helped, not even the fire from the disintegrator cannons. The gate did not budge.

The stranger was silent but they heard a hissing noise behind them. A blue-white ring of fire sprang up from the ground and surrounded the *Stardust*.

'Didn't I tell you that you'll burn in hell,' snarled the grim miscreant out of the past. Now Rhodan was ready to believe in his existence. 'Only three more minutes for you. You can't touch me, pardner, it's got to be done in my time.'

The men from the landing commando held their ground in front of the unkempt gunslinger, while Rhodan slowly retreated to the leading vehicle. The stranger watched him suspiciously. Rhodan leaned against the open door and folded his hands behind his back.

'Only in your time, you mean?' Rhodan said icily.

Something could be glimpsed coming from behind Rhodan's back, causing the stranger to make a fast draw. A sharp crack from a Colt shattered the quiet and black smoke billowed up. Simultaneously, the outcast spun about before falling to the ground.

In Rhodan's hand glistened the gun found by Everson. The victim, gunned down under such baffling circumstances, vanished into thin air. A wailing sound like soft crying persisted for a short time, then everything was over.

The curtain of energy before the portal was obliterated and the ring of fire around the *Stardust* died down.

Breathing heavily, Rhodan leaned on the vehicle. The old weapon dangled from his trigger finger.

'There's the key lying on the ground,' Rhodan

said impatiently. 'What are you waiting for? That rascal was no fake. *He* collared him in the 19th century and surrounded him with an impenetrable energy screen. When he said that he is invulnerable except in his own time, I remembered the old gun which I had put on the seat next to me. Everson, if you hadn't found that old shooting iron in the grass, who knows ... !'

Rhodan, feeling exhausted, fell silent. The encounter with the awakened dead from the past had been nerve-racking.

Seconds later the portal opened. An impulse from the key was sufficient to unlock it.

'Welcome, come in!' a deep voice intoned. This time it really sounded acoustic, not just a suggestion implanted in the subconscious mind.

'Hello, old friend,' Rhodan greeted, waving his hand. 'That interlude with the Colt wasn't such a bad joke. The gentleman has a thrilling sense of humor.'

Khrest was outraged by Rhodan's banter. He looked anxiously around until the bellowing cascades of laughter broke out again. It was as if *he* wanted to set the whole artificial planet vibrating with his howling laughter.

Rhodan leaned his back against the wall. With a fixed smile on his face he surveyed the expansive hall behind the portal. They had reached their goal!

NINE

CONFRONTATION WITH – *IT!*

It was not a human being. *It* was no organic being at all. Perhaps *it* had once had a body until *it* became tired of it in the course of millions of years and freed *itself* of the troublesome burden.

Hence, the one-time organism had developed into *It*. Nevertheless, *it* could be seen if *it* so decided.

'What is *it*?' Rhodan had asked.

John Marshall, the sensitive telepath, understood his boss despite the raucous laughter. Marshall had been listening for a long time to the unending laughter. Finally he conversed telepathically with Betty Toufry.

He or *it* was so exhilarated that the gales of laughter kept continuing. Something must have happened, or it was something Rhodan had said, which was a source of great amusement.

Finally, Marshall shouted into Rhodan's ear:

'*It* is an interconnected entity, the living psyche of a supra-dimensional collective being, made up of billions of individual minds. You might think of it as an entire race having given up its material form in order to live on spiritually. We have here a voluntary denial of bodily existence after an inconceivably long span of life which the organism in its material form in all probability had become unable to endure any longer. It is *It!* Regardless of whether it represents billions of dematerialized brains or only one: it is *It.*'

Rhodan held his head with both hands. Marshall could not stifle a smile as he read his commander's thought.

'I'm sane, I swear I'm sane!' Rhodan had shouted.

The laughter was suddenly stilled. It had become very quiet in the huge, high-domed hall which seemed to contain nothing but a few nondescript machines.

They stood about twenty yards from the entrance and looked into the empty space which was permeated by a vague pink light.

This changed immediately as a certain form spontaneously took shape. It occurred in the exact center under the cupola.

A bright flash erupted from the ceiling. Moments later, undulating vapors formed high above the floor and became spirals which finally coalesced into a slowly rotating ball.

'Welcome,' the same voice reverberated through the hall. 'You might consider my appearance somewhat unusual. However, by now you should have learned not to expect the ordinary from me.'

A subdued laughter followed.

Perry Rhodan was momentarily seized by a feeling of loneliness. Khrest and Thora stood well ahead of the waiting men. Khrest's face was turned upward toward where the voice came from.

Rhodan still leaned with both shoulders against the cold metal wall, thinking grimly:

'Get this confounded nonsense over with. I've got more important things to do than to prolong an old man's life. How much longer will it take?'

'Please step a little closer!' the voice requested.

Rhodan pushed his cap back. He looked with sleepless red eyes at Khrest who moved solemnly forward.

'I'm green with envy,' Bell whispered. 'I wonder if *it* bestows the cell conservation on him?'

'Of course,' Rhodan murmured wearily. 'Why do you think we've been tested so rigorously? I can't believe that *it* would go back on *its* word now. I'd really like to know two things: first, why *it* wants to give away its secret, and second, when I can get some sleep. That's all.'

'Step a little closer, please,' the demand was repeated.

Unsure, Khrest looked around. He already stood close to the pulsating, flowing image in which Marshall believed he saw the amalgamation of multifarious and concentrated mind impulses of dematerialized intelligent beings.

Rhodan, tired of the whole affair, pointed forward with his thumb.

'Go on, go on!' he called irritatedly. 'Or do you want me to carry you under the light?'

Khrest shuddered. He dared one more step. Then he uttered a loud scream as an invisible

118

force hurled him back so that he helplessly fell against Thora.

'It wasn't you I meant, Arkonide, I'm sorry to say,' the voice was heard again. 'I've already given your race a chance 20,000 years ago by your count. I cannot grant you, as the representative of a degenerated race, the secret of biological prolongation of life. The time you had has come to an end.'

Khrest was still sobbing. Rhodan's shoulders slowly jerked away from the wall as if in a spasm.

'Hey!' was all Bell could utter, whirling around. Rhodan looked into his wide-open eyes.

'Hello, old friend, why don't you come closer?' someone said laughingly. 'We already know each other, don't we?'

Rhodan could feel his knees wobble. His face was white as chalk, contrasting sharply with the dark stubble of his beard.

'Step forward, sir!' Betty Toufry urged him. 'You were meant, not the pathetic old man.'

The men from the landing commando moved back deferentially. The utter disbelief in their faces was replaced by undisguised enthusiasm and admiration.

Only Rhodan failed to understand the ramifications.

'Just a minute,' he mumbled lamely. 'I assumed you ...'

Rhodan felt himself lifted up gently and carried under the lighted sphere which descended until it was at the level of Rhodan's face.

'Well, that's what he looks like,' mused the somber voice. 'An unostentatious, impetuous native from a small planet in a little solar system. Let me see now. He is thoughtful and a dreamer, free of self-indulgence and demanding self-discipline in others. He is idealistic and constructive. It is his desire to achieve greatness, but he doesn't realize what it is. In order to fulfill his aim, he reaches for me. Hello, old friend!'

Rhodan regained his mental alertness as the booming laughter shook the hall for the third time.

Suddenly he experienced a revelation of what he confronted. He was in the presence of the quintessence of serenity, maturity and selfless denial.

Rhodan was stirred by Pucky's high-pitched comment:

'Now I know, chief. *It* likes to play as much as I do, but *it* plays differently. *It* plays with you, with time and what you call cultural epochs. Do you understand me?'

Yes, Rhodan had finally attained full comprehension. The laughter became even louder after Pucky's remarks.

Rhodan felt exhausted. He hardly dared consider what he was offered by the omnipotent dematerialized being.

What was this 'chance' the Arkonides had been given 20,000 years ago?

Rhodan waited until it was quiet again before he proceeded to ask a question which startled the listening men:

'Hello, old friend, you put a monster aboard my ship. Do you remember?'

'I remember everything I've ever done,' asserted the incredible being with amusement.

'Okay,' Rhodan demanded, 'then will you please see to it that we won't have to amputate the arm of the injured navigator. The beast was highly poisonous and we don't have any anti-serum on board. This is the most important problem for me at present.'

There was a silence and a sensation as if the entire artificial planet commenced to breathe. Rhodan looked wryly at the flickering light. Khrest had fainted in the aftermath of the shock he had suffered. Thora stood with closed eyes at the wall. She realized that the Arkonides had lost their last hope.

All had been in vain; the expedition, the alliance with humans and many other efforts. *It* rejected the Arkonides as losers. *It* was intransigent and uncompromising.

'What do you have in mind, my friend?' the voice inquired calmly.

'Help for my injured technician first of all!'

'The cure is on the way. The poison will be extracted from the body. And you, my friend, you wish to take over the Arkonide Imperium? You'd like to rebuild it, restore order and pacify it, wouldn't you?'

'You know my innermost thoughts,' Rhodan admitted with a sigh.

'Many have aspired to it before you. Most of them have already failed at my second task; they are always the same. I've seen highly civilized cultures come and go. I've guided some of them till I lost interest. Perhaps I have a need for diversion. There was another race before the Arkonides, and another one prior to that. I've taken a good look at your world, Perry Rhodan. I'm willing to give you and people like you the same chance the Arkonides had. It is only a moment for me, then I'll have to wait again for someone who can grasp the meaning of the clues I scatter all over, someone to devote himself to their pursuit. I thank you for the amusing game, my friend. You've given a splendid account of yourself. Go to work now! I won't assist you nor will I oppose you. Enter the physiotron. The technical aids of my artificial world will be at your disposal. However, you'll have to find out for yourself what you can accomplish with them. Are we agreed?'

'It's a deal!' Rhodan exclaimed.

It laughed once again, this time its laugh tinged with melancholy. The soft voice concluded, slowly fading away:

'You expect immortality to be something great and beautiful? All organic beings harbor this thought, only to experience a sad disappointment. The last escape is dematerialization. One day you'll be glad to free your mind from its confining body. But there is plenty of time for you, at least in your own terms. Good luck, old friend! I've played with you the most thrilling game since I gave up my material existence. I'll continue to observe you. Good luck!'

The spiral of light was gone and the vast hall was empty again.

Before the spectators could say anything, a man appeared from nowhere.

'I've been assigned to you,' the new arrival said matter-of-factly. 'Please, choose a name for me!'

'Who are you?' Rhodan asked with dry lips. The stranger, who looked like a human being, smiled.

'I've been created for you, sir, hence my human form.'

'Are you a robot?'

'In a manner of speaking, yes, but not a machine in the ordinary sense. My brain is a half organic and half intotronic blend.'

'Intotronic?' Rhodan echoed.

'Six-dimensional, sir. Would you care to enter the physiotron now?'

'Why? What is it?'

'A cell spray, sir. You've probably assumed that the biological conservation is effected by injection or radiation, but this would be erroneous. May I explain to you that you'll receive a conservation charge for each cell unit lasting exactly sixty-two years on your time scale. Subsequently, it will be followed by instantaneous decay unless you return here before the expiration of the allotted period in order to receive a renewed dose.'

'Every sixty-two years?' Rhodan muttered. His

mind was gradually becoming confused.

'Yes, sir. I must advise you, however, that you'll always have to find this planet yourself when you desire it. I'll be at your disposal anytime together with all the means extant here but you'll have to come to me. Would you please enter now? Time is getting short.'

The portent of the last remark was only much later understood by Rhodan.

*   *   *

It was a short but intense pain, compared to which a great transition felt harmless.

Rhodan's body was transformed into a nebulous thin cloud inside the heavy metal column. It lasted more than an hour, Bell later claimed.

The strange robot stood motionlessly at the controls of a machine which defied understanding by the average human mind.

Rhodan's dematerialized substance was exposed to the internal force fields. One could only imagine the complicated process involved in the treatment, but it eluded real comprehension.

If *it* had any intent to do so, *it* could easily set *itself* up as ruler of the Galaxy.

However, *it* no longer entertained such an idea. Maybe *it* had earlier been tempted by this ambition. Now, *it* merely played a role in the background. *Its* demands were modest.

Whoever succeeded in passing the devised tests, was rewarded with a chance for a period of 20,000

CONFRONTATION WITH – IT!

years. It was a reasonable chance but it all depended on how it was used.

After the procedure Rhodan awoke in the same state of fatigue in which he had stepped into the machine. Silently, he dressed again.

He cast a searching and somewhat suspicious glance at the humanoid attending him.

'Was this a rejuvenation?' Rhodan asked dubiously. 'It felt more like a hyper-transition.'

'It wasn't supposed to rejuvenate you, sir,' he replied. 'I had instructions to conserve you in your present state. From now on you'll age no more. You'll remain at the phase you've reached at the moment.'

'This I'll have to see! How is the injured man getting along?'

'He's well again. We apologize. May I ask you to come to the programmer? All aggregates on this planet will have to be tuned to your individual vibrations. Your time is running out, sir. By the way, you may designate any other person you wish to undergo a cell conservation. You have the power to use all the equipment on this planet as you choose. Do you have any special requests?'

Rhodan's eyes swept over the suddenly tense faces of his companions. With a bitter feeling he noticed their inordinate desire.

Of course, it was the natural expression of a deeply ingrained striving. Who would have refused a cell conservation!

Rhodan realized at this moment that he would

always retain the loyalty of his companions. Only he could grant them access to the physiotron.

'Bell, get in!' Rhodan said gruffly. Then he left the hall following behind the human robot.

*   *   *

As *Stardust II* prepared for hyper-transition, the ersatz sun, a true replica of a natural star, faded away far behind the rocket's flaming exhausts. The planet Wanderer diminished in the distance.

The shock of transition struck like a physical blow. When the battleship emerged once more in normal space, Vega was burning brightly before it, a familiar celestial beacon.

Rhodan glanced briefly at the observation screens. Vega was quiescent again; no trace of a developing nova could be detected in the great star. *It* had kept *its* promise: Vega, which had been forced into an eruptive state in the course of one of the Immortal's manifold tasks, was once again internally stabilized. It was useless to speculate about the incredible fact; their brains were not of an order advanced enough to comprehend the complex superscience necessary to control the energies of a sun.

Rhodan was exhausted from the recent ordeal. 'A short stop-over on Ferrol,' he ordered, then transferred command to Maj. Nyssen. The pilots of the Arkonide fighter crafts saluted their commander. Khrest and Thora had already silently retired to their cabins.

To himself Perry added, 'I wonder why the mentanical was in such a hurry?' But the human-oid servant of *it* had remained on far distant Wanderer and its six-dimensional brain was not about to satisfy Perry's intellectual curiosity.

Alone, Rhodan reflected. The recognition the Immortal had granted him left him awestruck with its implications. With that single supramundane act a new era had been initiated. Phase I of the Space Age had ended and Phase II had begun. Soon all mankind would begin to think and operate not in national, global or even interplanetary terms but in stellar; interstellar terms.

All the universe beckoned.